APRIL COTTAGE

Pam Jones

With

Richard Shemilt

Edited by
Richard Shemilt

April Cottage

Pam Jones with Richard Shemilt
Edited by Richard Shemilt

This novel is a work of fiction. Names and characters are the product of the author's imagination and any resemblance to actual persons, living or dead, is entirely coincidental.

First edition 2017.

Published independently 2017.
Printed by Amazon.

ISBN: 9781549671722

APRIL COTTAGE

For Ron

-Out in the fields with God-

APRIL COTTAGE

APRIL COTTAGE

'I have been here before

But when or how I cannot tell;

I know the grass beyond the door;

The sweet keen smell.'

-D. G. Rossetti

APRIL COTTAGE

APRIL COTTAGE

PROLOGUE

Somewhere over Germany
October 1942

"We're on fire! The wing's burning!"

The young Flying-officer screamed out in terror to the rest of his crew aboard the bomber; plummeting towards the ground through burning flames and searing heat. He continued calling in anguish from the cockpit to the rear-turrets, but the enemy blast had silenced everybody aboard that plane except for one. He sat staring at the lifeless controls, petrified with fear inside the violently shaking fuselage.

Suddenly, the fear was swept aside and time seemed to slow down. He was no longer in his own body as he looked up through the cockpit window towards the cloudy sky. The clouds were twisting and transforming into images with mercurial obscurity. The images were familiar. Images of his own life – literally passing before his eyes – and finally; a face. A beautiful woman's face appearing in the clouds, calling out to him.

His wife's face. He remembered the words he'd said to her only hours ago before leaving her for his routine flight over foreign soil.

"No goodbyes, sweetheart. No goodbyes - because I'm coming back to you. To *both* of you. That's a promise!"

With a new surge of fear, he was back in his own body, terrified. There was nothing he could do except look at the ground, which was flying towards him at an alarming rate. Seconds before impact, he shielded his eyes – and then there was nothing.

He found himself standing amongst the twisted metal wreckage of the bomber on the ashen, charred pastureland. There was no sound, only lifeless silence as he involuntarily drifted away from the scene into complete darkness towards a strange, bright light, somewhere in the distance.

APRIL COTTAGE

APRIL COTTAGE

APRIL COTTAGE

1

Staffordshire, England
April 1990

 Fresh from the firing line of the Friday-night chat-show and still fighting fit, Guy Anderson smirked with a certain amount of conceit as he boomed his Jaguar XJ-S into fifth along the northbound carriageway of England's M1 motorway. Cameras had zoomed in and the studio audience had warmly appreciated the way the well-known actor had derisively zapped the questions when the conversation had predictably changed course; one minute he was being allowed to plug his brilliant starring role in a new play, and the next he was facing interrogations surrounding his private affairs. He'd been blatantly forewarned however, that in view of recent press revelations certain questions were naturally unavoidable – the whole thing would have made for dull and pointless viewing if he wasn't prepared to put himself in the hot seat.

His triumphant grin flashed at the windscreen as he recalled the guarded exchanges; flippant responses to a barrage of meaningful quips and queries had brought generous and supportive applause plus an unusual amount of sweat to the brow of the beaming, yet squirming interviewer. But now, in the face of an onslaught of piercing headlights, growing irritation changed his grin to a grimace as, having made the interchange to the M6, he now cruised with uncertainty towards his destination.

"Where in God's name is the Potteries?" Anderson muttered.

As far as he was concerned, the five towns were long-lost in a whirl of pot-bank smog and the fictitious world of Arnold Bennett. Why on Earth Stoke-on-Trent had been selected for the last stop of the play's provincial tour, he'd never know; it certainly wasn't much of a stepping stone to the West-end run! *Who would expect to find a noteworthy theatre in such obscure territory?* But when the tour's production manager, Oberon Mercer, affectionately known as the *Fairy-Queen*, had rung his Kensington apartment earlier in the day he'd been assured that there was in fact not one, but two theatres of note in the area – the prestigious Theatre Royal, plus a rather splendid theatre-in-the-round!

Oberon Mercer's wheedling words were still fresh in Guy's mind. It was a welcome distraction from the long, tedious drive

"And I am informed," Mercer persisted, "There are plans for a much grander theatre - to be known as *The Regent* - which tells me, Guy love, that Stoke-on-Trent *must* have a very healthy theatre-going public!"

There was a brief pause.

"And what's more..." Oberon concluded, "It's a great big-fat sell-out! You're packing 'em in!"

Hardly surprising, Guy had thought with hackles rising again; after all, his name had been scandalously splashed across every tabloid in the country. "The morons will be turning out in droves, merely to gloat!" he'd responded.

"Leave the M6 and follow signs for Stoke-on-Trent" the camp cajolement had continued. "I'll meet you at the Five Towns hotel as we planned; I'll have a meal waiting for you – they do a good steak! You can't miss it, it's just across the road from the railway station – the rest of the cast have booked in here as it's no distance from the theatre. And don't worry, Guy love; they've found you a nice little place on the VIP dig's list. April Cottage! It's five miles out into the countryside; sounds like the perfect retreat. So, Guy love, break-a-leg with the interview tonight! We'll all be watching in from my room!"

Guy had then envisaged the small company of fellow-actors traipsing along the hotel corridors to Oberon's room for a communal gawp at the tube. Good old Henry, fat cigar in hand, would be heavily slumped into the only comfortable armchair. Kat, Max and Rodney would be youthfully stretched-out over the carpet. Oberon, wafting away the cigar smoke, would be delicately perched on the edge of his bed with the long-suffering Ronnie; having been invited to share the perch, cautiously distancing himself away on the opposite side, and of course the lovely Dee would have draped her elegant self into the background, pretending not to be interested. Guy rolled his eyes at the predictable nature of his colleagues and with a wry smile, lowered his foot on the accelerator. Every fibre in his body could feel the velocity of the 5.0 litre V12 engine as he fired towards his destination, leaving nothing but an abundance of carbon emissions and burnt rubber in the heat haze of his trail.

2

The dashboard's digital clock was approaching the twenty-three-hour figure as Anderson freely accelerated along the fast-lane. April Cottage, no matter how delightful, would have to wait until morning. Tonight, regardless of his loathing for hotels, he resigned himself to a one-night stay at the Five Towns hotel with the rest of the cast.

If there were no rooms available he could doss down with someone; providing it wasn't Oberon! As for Dee – he had no doubt that she would be more than accommodating; it was painfully obvious to him that she was itching to give him her own brand of sex and sympathy now that Roxanne had publicly ditched him after fifteen years of marriage. And for what? *A bloody toy-boy!* And worse; she'd blown the lot to some bitch-of-a-gossip-columnist who'd seized the reins with maximum force, racing her off into the headlines on both sides of the Atlantic. Guy was all too familiar with gossip and could turn a blind eye in that direction, but this was different and he still smarted from the whiplash of the printed word.

Headlined *the Anderson Split*, the trite bit of journalism had read like a paragraph from some cheap novel:

'Flashing her dark eyes and tossing back those famous dark tresses, Roxanne moved her hips against the young blonde Adonis towering at her side. Claiming him with possessive and unshakable adoration she finally and ruthlessly exploded any myth that the Andersons were, as often reported, inseparable. I'd put it to her straight, why ditch the handsome Guy Anderson for a toy-boy? 'He may be handsome!' she'd snapped, 'but he's a complete waste-of-space in the bedroom!'

"The bitch! The insensitive little bitch!" he hissed the words as the blood rushed to his face and his foot angrily pushed on the gas pedal. The speedometer swung crazily to the hundred-mark as the oncoming signs for Stoke-on-Trent appeared, forcing him to slow down. He was shortly facing signs for the city centre and railway station.

A shadowy row of cars stood in front of the floodlit hotel; one of them being Oberon's yellow Beetle, smattered with posters of the play and predominantly parked with a convenient space alongside. Guy popped out to remove the reserved marker-board before returning to ease the XJS into position. As he locked the Jag, he paused to survey the city street, which was incredibly as he'd imagined it would be; drab and lifeless except for a single taxi-cab driving noiselessly by. He turned to gaze up at the hotel. It was the usual imposing type of building with a timeworn brick façade that would have once welcomed only the most eminent of railway visitors to the pottery town.

The revolving doors whisked him into a spaciously elegant foyer, where glass-fronted display units exhibited a chosen array of notable brands of earthenware and china. He'd long been accustomed to the startled hush that suddenly descended whenever he entered a public place. Despite the late hour this was no exception, although it was only members of staff who seemed aware of his presence. He strode across the carpeted foyer to face the look of recognition now registering on the young, male receptionist's face.

"Oh good-evening, sir. I saw you on the telly tonight!"

Another figure suddenly appeared behind the desk, quickly ushering the receptionist aside.

"Thank you, Malcolm, I'll take care of this." The man whispered in a dismissive tone, before turning toward Anderson. "Welcome to the Five Towns hotel, sir. I'm the manager of this fine establishment and it gives me the utmost pleasure to extend a very personal welcome to you. If you would care to have a late meal, we have a table reserved for you in the Royal-Doulton restaurant. I understand that Mr. Oberon Mercer is waiting there for you to join him."

"That's right, thanks. By the way, I need a room; just for tonight."

"A room, sir?"

"Yep. Anything will do."

"But I was given to understand that you wouldn't be staying here?"

"It's a bit late to go anywhere else now so if you can arrange something, I'll be off in the morning."

The manager engineered a hurried smile. "But of course, sir. We shall be only too pleased to accommodate you, and may I say - for as long as you wish!"

"As I said, it will be fine just for the one night, thanks."

"The Wedgewood-suite would have been eminently suitable but I regret to say it is occupied at present; I can offer you the Minton-room instead, sir?"

"Thanks, anything will do. I could sleep on the floor tonight!"

"I shall see to it that the Minton-room is prepared for you immediately!"

The manager shot a meaningful glare at the eager-eyed receptionist, then left.

3

Two middle-aged matrons were hovering and sidling along the edge of the reception desk and casting furtive little glances at Guy whilst feigning interest in a pile of publicity leaflets. He satisfied their inane curiosity by dutifully smiling in their direction before escaping down the stretched, carpeted passage towards the sanctuary of the dimly-lit restaurant. It was a long room still retaining much of its Victorian grandeur and was likely now used for conferences and other social events.

Oberon, tucked away in a secluded corner – well away from the handful of late diners – rose like a phoenix from the flames.

"Guy love! At Last! Sit down; my God, you look like death!"

A waiter appeared to offer the menu. Guy waived it aside and asked for a rare fillet steak and salad with a bottle of Beaujolais.

"That was clever stuff you gave us on the box tonight!" Oberon beamed from beneath a fringe of bleached hair.

"Yep, but it's history now. Let's forget it."

The stage manager, slightly miffed, leaned back resignedly into the plush-backed dining chair remembering what a trauma it had all been. Over the pink table linen, he observed the tired face of Guy Anderson now staring into a vacuum of space. Hours earlier beneath the menacing glare of studio lights, those dark-haired masculine features had emanated the strong public-image, which thousands of women would have been waiting to see – and typically, he hadn't disappointed them. He'd flashed many an easy smile at the camera with the renowned ebony moustache suggestively tracing the curve of his upper lip. Sleek, dark eyebrows had hovered provocatively over those famous bedroom-eyes, which Oberon recalled, had been riveted on the interviewer with such tenacity. Now, in the gilt-edged gloom of this large and almost deserted room, this was the very private face of an ageing star.

Oberon Mercer, slightly Guy's senior, liked to think of himself as a mentor and one of his closest friends; he loved and respected this unassuming man who had never taken fame for granted and it was painful to see him having to bear the brunt of a backlash of bitter and suggestive statements, which had pointedly been aimed at harming his reputation. He was now feeling the strong urge to mother-and-console but knew that Guy would never be receptive to that kind of treatment from another man. For now, he could only look on with the deepest kind of affection.

Like a few others in the theatrical industry, Oberon knew that the Anderson marriage had become a total sham. Over the last few years since that long-lost glittering showbiz wedding he'd seen the opposing images; public and private, on-stage and off, the love and developing hate! The whole relationship had pulsated with dramatic incident, making it one big act – and now, the final curtain had been brought down with a bump. End of the whole sorry performance. It was a relief to all concerned; Roxanne was a silly little superficial actress who had been utterly spoiled, chiefly by Guy and he would be the first to admit it. His biggest mistake had been in finally thinking their union might be improved if they had a bash at working together. When he'd suggested her for the lead-role opposite him in this new play, everyone had told him it wouldn't work but he'd been utterly determined to give it a go and of course it had all ended, predictably, in disaster.

Roxanne had returned to the musical stage; where she belonged according to Oberon. She had since met this juvenile dancer whose *jetés* had lifted her off her tiny feet, sending her even tinier mind pirouetting into the direction of the international press.

The fillet steak was delivered with a crisp green salad and Guy didn't waste any time in tackling it.

"Would you care to taste the Beaujolais, Sir?" the waiter dutifully poured a drop into the glass.

"Try it, 'Bron, and if it's good – help yourself" Guy gestured.

"Perfection!" Oberon conveyed as he savoured the wine. "I'll have a quickie with you then I simply must retire – I'm desperate for sleep! I certainly don't envy you, Guy love, going off to some strange abode in the countryside at *this* time of night – but you will insist on cutting yourself off from the rest of us; which reminds me to give you this." He reached down into the pocket of his purple jeans. "Here – written directions from my own hand, to April Cottage."

"Forget it, I've booked in here for the night."

"Oh, so sensible! You'll have all the time in the world tomorrow to drive out there and settle in. Ronnie and I will be up at some obscene time in the morning so, in case I don't see you, you might as well have these directions to the cottage now – and here's the key; it weighs a ton!" He handed over the key and quickly rose to his feet. "And if you'll forgive me, Guy love, it's *beddybies* for me – or I shall never be up for the fray: the local amateurs have been in for the last few days with *Godspell*, the poor dears – and tomorrow night they'll be having their after-show fling with a strike to complete afterwards. I tremble to think how long it will take them to dismantle; I have visions of our set moving into the wings minutes before curtain-up! We all know what these amateurs are – elation and deflation! But have no fear, Ronnie and I will be there to sort the dears out and hopefully, we'll be set up for the technical rehearsal on Sunday."

Oberon raised from his seat.

"Oh, and there's a phone at the cottage so I can ring you with the time details. Monday night's prices are reduced at the box office, so that alone assures a first-night sell-out." Oberon insisted.

"What's the theatre like?" Guy pondered.

"Not bad. Large and draughty but traditional and I believe the acoustics are excellent. Needs a coat of paint in the corridors and the green-room leaves a bit to be desired but your dressing-room is quite respectable. It's better than the *Hippodrome*!"

"Anything would be better than the *Hippodrome*!"

"The Theatre Royal is getting on a bit, but the folk round here are sadly quite fond of it."

"Why 'sadly'?" Guy asked.

"Apparently it's under threat of closure to make way for a far grander place. There are big plans to rebuild the former Regent cinema into a first-class theatre. So, Guy love, next time we're here, it could be ready!"

"Next time? Are you kidding? I'll be resting by then!"

"The next time you rest, Guy Anderson, is when you're six-foot-under! And before then you'll have many more outstanding performances with a knighthood to match!" With that Oberon turned to make a flamboyant departure through a maze of deserted tables and chairs. Guy exhaled deeply, before continuing to indulge decadently in the refined cuisine before him – an idiosyncrasy of fame to which he'd become accustomed, but never took for granted.

4

The Minton-room was massive with one enormous bay-window overlooking the railway station. The buff-coloured walls were surmounted with an ornamental cornice and an abundance of oak-framed pictures, which gave the place all the charisma of a museum. A large crystal chandelier hung centrally, casting dismal shadows over the neatly spread counterpane on the king-size bed. The *en-suite* facilities, with a massive oak door ludicrously marked W.C. in gold lettering, were a well-preserved relic of the thirties. The enormous white bath had copper taps and the *Twyford's* lavatory basin had an antiquated wooden seat, which had been manufactured to impress – or to accommodate a very large bottom! Guy swilled his face at the pedestal bowl and, snatching a warm towel from the radiator, moved hastily back into the bedroom.

How he detested hotel rooms! And he'd been in the most sumptuous of apartments to the most squalid of bed-sits. He'd had a belly-full of board and bedding and endless wearisome nights between the sheets with, in the early days, only God knows who! That's why he now always insisted on the theatre administration finding him self-catering, out-of-town accommodation. Not only did such an arrangement seek to isolate him from the scrutiny of the public-eye, it also filled a great inner need to regain that quality of life long-lost somewhere in the memories of his rural upbringing. Even the dull prospect of going over lines was a joy when it could be done within the auditorium of an open field with a back-cloth of shaded hills, and a silent audience of sheep or cows. Indeed, none of the *glitz* in his highly successful lifestyle could remotely compare with a pre-theatre stroll down an English country-lane.

All of that would have to wait until tomorrow. Choosing to ignore the grotesque valet-stand his things were thrown over the back of a chair; sock and shoes went hurtling into space – missing the chandelier by inches. Finally, in boxer-shorts and a shirt, he fought off the restrictions of the tightly folded sheets and eventually lay staring up at a darkened ceiling until the sound of a passing train carried him away into the lap of Morpheus.

5

It was the rattle of the trains that woke him the following morning. He was soon up, dressed and down in the Bottle-oven grille having coffee and toast. A few businessmen were breakfasting and thankfully appeared not to notice that there was a celebrity amongst them; *probably didn't give a piss*, Guy thought approvingly.

Guy glanced through the front-window to notice the absence of the yellow Beetle, which meant that Oberon had already left for the theatre. Dee's black-topped mini was there, which prompted him to demolish his bit of buttered toast at treble speed. If there was one person he could do without seeing it was the delightful Dee, and there was a good chance of making a getaway before she or the rest of the cast arose.

Too late! He'd risen from his chair and turned to see the golden-haired Delia, standing in the doorway, staring across at him with raised eyebrows. She moved directly to his table.

"Guy! What on Earth are you doing here?"
"Nothing! I'm just leaving."

"Leaving? But you can't be! Sit down again and tell me what's going on." She flashed a command at the waitress. "Coffee for two, please!"

"Coffee for *one*, please!" Guy asserted admonishingly in Dee's direction.

"Two coffees please!" Dee reiterated waiving the confused girl aside. "Guy will you please stop looking at me like that and sit down!"

Hastening to avoid any further crescendo in her voice, Guy's bottom resignedly hit the chair.

"Okay, Guy. What's going on? Why on Earth didn't you let me know you were staying here?"

"I'm not staying here! I'm leaving! Right after the interrogation."

"Have you just arrived?"

"No, I got here last night."

"Last night? Why didn't you let me know?"

"Why should I let you know? Anyway, it was late, very late. You'd gone to bed."

"You could have rung my room. Guy, you look dreadful! You haven't even bothered to shave!"

"I'm growing a beard!" He said, grudgingly.

"Don't be ridiculous!"

The coffee arrived and Dee waited in dutiful silence until the waitress had poured it into the cups and left.

"Why didn't you ring my room last night?" She persisted.

"I've told you, it was late."

"You know that I wouldn't have given a shit how late it was!"

Dee only swore when she was irate, and hell was she irate. It was all there in those green eyes, which he explored every night when the two of them were locked together on the hideous floral settee at centre-stage; with a massed fusion of faces looking silently on from the rows of darkened seats beyond. Those green eyes, always so expressive in making her innermost desires known to him.

He knew most men would have fallen over backwards to oblige, but she didn't want most men – she wanted him. He, however, wasn't prepared to entangle himself in another theatrical relationship; not now, and ideally, not ever!

"The television interview went well." She said it calmly, having lit one of her gold-tipped menthols and disregarding the no-smoking sign. "It's time this nation heard the other side of the coin. You did it so well; it will be a real smack in the eye for that ex-wife of yours!"

The green eyes narrowed to slits as she exhaled smoke into the air. They drank their coffee in silence for a moment or two. As always, she was the first to speak.

"I merely wanted to congratulate you, Guy, and I'm sorry if…"

Relenting, he touched her hand across the table, giving her one of those famous lingering smiles.

"I know, and Thanks." Guy pushed his chair back and rose to his feet. "See you at the theatre tomorrow, for the tech."

"Guy…" she began plaintively and he knew what was coming. "I'm not doing anything today. There's no performance this evening and there's absolutely nothing for me to do in this dump of a town. They tell me there's a football match on and the place will be swarming with fans. Max and Rodney are taking Kat and I'll be here on my own. Can't I come with you? 'Bron said they've found you a darling little cottage in the countryside. Please, Guy, let me come with you?"

This was precisely what he'd been trying to avoid. He sat down again.

"Look, Dee, no offence, but if you don't mind I really do need to be on my own for a while."

"But I do mind, damn you!"

"Then for once in your life you will have to be very understanding. I need a little solitude, that's all. I need to think things over – on my own."

"But I wouldn't…"

"On my own!" Guy snorted with a certain decisiveness.

"Alright!" She acknowledged, huskily inhaling smoke. "If I want to avoid being crushed to death by a great mob of soccer hooligans, I'll simply have to shut myself in my room for the day!"

"Now *you're* being ridiculous, Dee! They won't come near this place!"

"Won't they!?" Dee asked, stubbing her cigarette emphatically into the saucer. "I should imagine hordes of them will be arriving here by train! And don't forget, darling, the railway station is just across the road!"

"I think you'll find they go directly to the ground by coach. Get out before they come. You've got a car! Explore the five towns – the shops should be pretty good – bursting with a choice of pottery I should imagine."

"And who wants pottery?" She sulked.

"Look, Dee, the day will be gone before you know it." Guy rose, moving round to her side of the table, leaning over to murmur in her ear. "And then it will just be a matter of time before we'll be back together, on stage, sharing that sexy little clinch." He kissed her ear to seal the promise.

Her face was motionless. "What you don't realise, darling Guy, is that you and I could have so much more excitement off-stage!"

"Of that I have no doubt!" He squeezed her hand and made a swift exit.

6

With Oberon's carefully written instructions propped upon the dashboard, Guy was soon cruising down a succession of busy motor lanes. With the pottery towns now behind him, he was suddenly uplifted by the inviting way ahead where hawthorn hedges were besieged with tiny cream buds already nodding into blossom.

With the pressure of flowing traffic gone he could now drive at a more leisurely pace as he went in search of April Cottage. He mused on the name, breathing it, uttering it and finding a kind of comfort in doing so. *April Cottage*, such an apt destination in this first week of April.

He thought of Dee sitting alone in her room at the hotel and a surge of guilt swept over him. He knew how desperately she wanted to be with him; but why take her for a ride? He didn't want her. He didn't want any woman. They were *two-a-penny*.

I suppose that makes me a bit of a bastard, he thought – but was quick to redeem himself. *I don't intend to be. All I want is a little space; a little peace! God knows why, but that's it.*

Guy Anderson was a name that lingered on the lips of thousands of women and he'd never been able to understand why? He didn't see himself as a sex symbol but, for some strange reason, they did; with looks of adulation in their eyes they clamoured to meet him at every opportunity. This had all stemmed from his days in New York when he'd first played Broadway. Those American women hadn't given him a moment to himself – one in particular – Roxanne! She'd bowled him over like a ten-pin. He was thirty-two then and she, stunningly attractive, half-Mexican and eight years his junior, was appearing in a bubbling all-black musical on the Great-White-way.

He'd been staying in a swish apartment at *The Pierre*; a Fifth-Avenue hotel reputed to have been favoured by Clark Gable to whom he apparently bore some resemblance; a fact he'd been made painfully aware of after returning home from the theatre one evening. He'd been embarrassingly accosted by some heavily jewelled matron who'd almost thrown herself at his feet in her declaration that as long as he lived, the *Hollywood King* would never be dead!

"I should know! I've seen every damn film that Gable ever made!" she'd boasted.

Frankly, not wanting to *give a damn*, Guy escaped the ambush by hastily stepping into the elevator as it conveniently paused to open its doors and, there she was – Roxanne! The doors closed. The lift took off, and suddenly they'd found themselves being elevated to heights far beyond those of the great Manhattan skyline.

That was fifteen tempestuous years ago and now his raven-haired beauty of an ex-wife had flown away with a twenty-four-year-old ballet-dancer. *Good luck to 'em! ...And Wolfgang Whatever-your-name-is, if you want kids – forget it! She hates 'em!*

Guy caught a glimpse of his own wistful expression in the car-mirror. He'd always wanted a little girl. Always. A frilly dressed toddler to dangle on his knee; a child to make everything he'd achieved worthwhile. He could so easily have been a father, but no! Something deep inside of him had longed for a daughter to come out of the marriage, but Roxanne had never agreed. There was nothing physically wrong with either of them – quite the reverse. He was as *fit-as-a-fiddle* and she was as rhythmic as a rhumba when it came to sex – but to her, the prevention of pregnancy had always been paramount. It was something he'd never been able to fathom without been subjected to a volcanic eruption of hot-blooded Mexican aggression, which had ranted of the hardships of being just one of a very large family with a long-suffering outsized momma giving her entire life to nurturing her offspring. Roxanne had screamed her hatred of motherhood and repeatedly foresworn that no breast-sucking brat was ever going to hang onto her.

After the long, steady decline of their marriage; rock-bottom had been reached and she'd spilled the Mexican beans in public, declaring him to be a waste-of-space in the bedroom. Even if that *were* based on the truth, to hear it openly declared in public by your ex was humiliating! According to his concerned agent, the whole thing could do harm to his professional image.

The strange thing about it was that it seemed to have the opposite effect. Apparently, numerous letters from irate women had been sent to all branches of the media; all set to prove Roxanne wrong – many stating that if only they were given the opportunity, they'd be more than happy to prove that he would be anything but a waste-of-space in their bed!

Thank the Lord he was inaccessible to them, after all, he was no fool. He knew these women merely needed someone to fulfil their fantasies. His real threat was the golden-haired Delia Davidson, who; because she claimed him once-nightly on the stage, assumed it gave her the God-given right to claim him twice-nightly!

7

Oberon's instructions led him to a narrow country lane, which set his heart racing with anticipation. *Let's hope this is just a taste of what's ahead for me,* he thought, before having to suddenly brake rather forcibly, as a thumping-great tractor was trundling towards him with a huge trailer in its wake. The man behind the wheel was mouthing and gesturing his annoyance at the alien vehicle daring to confront him. There was no alternative route for Guy – he had to reverse his jag into a gateway several metres back. The tractor drew up alongside and the ruddy-faced farmer leaned out of his cab to leer down at him.

"Posh car that, to bring down an *owd* cow-lane like this!" The farmer interrogated, in a strange, colloquial local dialect that Guy could barely understand.

"Suppose it *is* a bit off the beaten track. I'm looking for a place called April Cottage. Do you know it?"

"Know it? Course ah do, and ah knows you too don't ah?

"Do you?" Guy answered with contrived innocence.

"I've seen yer somewhere! Never forget a face me, never! Half-a-mo! Ah got it! The cattle-market! You're one of them auctioneers, right? Ah can spot 'em a mile off!"

"You amaze me!" Guy toyed, with sarcasm.

"Posh car, collar and tie job with an accent to match. Easy!"

"Hang on…" Guy replied whimsically. "Tractor and trailer, bib and brace job with green wellington boots; I've got it, *you're* a farmer!"

The farmer wasn't amused. "So, it's going on the market at last then?" He grimaced.

"What is?" Guy asked.

"April Cottage, of course…I take it that's what's brought you out here on a Saturday morning? Well, some poor bugger has got a load on his hands, that's all I can say!"

"Why do you say that?" Guy said with alarm bells sounding in his ears.

"You'll find out when yer get there. Come to do an evaluation on it have yer?"

"Not exactly." Guy said, guardedly.

"Been a nice little cottage in its day. I remember it back in the forties; well-kept, and the prettiest garden you've ever seen. I'll tell you something, folk knew how to keep a place nice in those days."

"Not so nice now then?"

"No." He pulled himself back into his cab. "No, sir. I think you've got yer work cut out to get yer sale-price for that one. They've been renting it out for a year or two. Landlords don't give a sod as long as they keep raking in the money. They doesn't have to put up with the worry of folk coming to the farm for milk and eggs and 'taters. Always close on milking-time they come, then go and leave the gates open behind 'em. Townies! I hate 'em! They know *nowt* about country matters, *nowt*! So, get yer sale-boards up and get it sold and we'll all be happy!"

Without another word, he revved-up the noisy engine and the tractor moved on up the lane. Guy gazed into the car-mirror, watching the trundling tractor and trailer disappear around the bend. With his preconception of April Cottage somewhat dented, he sat pondering in the car. Even *his* vagrant spirit didn't fancy seven nights in a tumbledown shack. He wondered, for a moment, whether to head back to the theatre and demand that the administration sort it out, after all; it was their duty, but upon reflection, they'd never let him down on the tour before and he was in striking-distance. Perhaps he should at least take a look at April Cottage.

8

Moving on to the end of the lane he joined a wider road and was soon passing through a hamlet, sign-posted *Whitemoor*, which was clearly defined in 'Bron's instructions. There was a rigid row of red-bricked terraced houses, one of them being a small shop. *Could be useful*, he thought. At the end of the row was a small hillock with the tiniest of churches and as he passed by, his attention was mystically drawn towards it. A kind of *déjà vu* moment.

Driving away from the hamlet, he continued past a small white-walled farmhouse with its hay-barn and cow-dotted field. Could that be the home of his newfound farmer-friend, he wondered as he drove up a tree-lined slope with very pleasant views on either side. This led to another downward slope where a sudden view of the landscape forced him to catch his breath so sharply that his feet hit the clutch and brake simultaneously, slowing his car down to a crawl.

The strangest of feelings came over him as his eyes riveted themselves over the spread of wooded fields below. It was as if a picture from the channel of his memory had been vividly sketched and brought to life. The road before him disappeared at the bottom of the slope where a crumbling stone wall rounded a sharp bend. He knew instinctively, without checking his instructions, that around the bend there was going to be a turn-off for a no-through road, which would take him to the end of his journey - and there, just as he'd expected, an old, leafy lane with a deeply-rooted finger-post-sign stating: 'No Thoroughfare'.

Guy steered the car into the lane where the raised shape of the lone, grey twin-chimney cottage beckoned to him as he now knew it would. It was unnervingly, shatteringly and frighteningly familiar. The car crunched to a crawl, over gravel, until it was alongside the five stone steps, which jutted out like talons from the bedraggled hedgerow. Perched above was a small hanging gate with a weather-worn board displaying two words that were barely visible: April Cottage.
He stayed in the car, with the engine switched off, for several minutes – peering up at the front hedge where masses of ivy trailed down to the ditches below. He couldn't see the house from where he sat, since it was set back, high off the lane. Taking the massive iron key from the glove compartment, his fingers closed over the

solid weight of metal; then cold and inanimate it lay on his open palm as he stared at it. There was something oddly familiar about that too!

9

From the top of the five stone steps, his curious gaze stretched over the overgrown garden to the cottage itself. Its yellowing walls were shrouded by a heavy shelf of showering ivy. Guy stared rather blankly at the central front-door with its wooden portal arrangement and, for some inexplicable reason, he half-expected someone to be waiting there to greet him.

He wandered along the narrow pathway, pausing where the twisting trunk of an old apple tree, sprouting the beginnings of its pink blossom, sank into the depths of an entanglement of weeds. Here and there a few daffodils had pushed their way through, whilst scattered clumps of struggling lupin plants were the only visible remnants of what would have been a once cared-for herbaceous border. The odd triangular shape of the garden was encompassed by a rambling privet hedge thrusting itself at acute angles noticeably at the point where the hanging gate hovered over the steps down to the lane.

Walking with uncertainty on towards the doorway it became very clear, very quickly, that the farmer hadn't been jesting; some poor bugger certainly had got a job on here! *What a sin to let it fall into this...shambles!* All thoughts of staying there had already been dismissed; there was absolutely no way he could stay here! Someone back at theatre-administration had a hell of a lot to answer for! *April Cottage on the VIP list? What kind of April-fool do they take me for?*

It was at that very moment when something caused Guy to abandon his thoughts. With a sharp, sudden intake of breath, he turned his attention to a movement at the latticed window. Someone was in there! *This house is supposed to be empty!?* Controlling himself, Guy moved nearer to the window, peering into what was now an empty room, before collecting his thoughts and convincing himself that what he thought he'd seen was merely a strand of hanging ivy swinging in the gentle breeze.

Lowering his six-foot frame to avoid the arched beam, he stepped into the sunlit porchway where dewy cobwebs glistened from corner to corner, spreading their silken finery across the creviced latch on the oak-framed door. The heavy key turned easily in the lock, but to gain entrance Guy had to push hard against the warped woodwork before finding himself at the bottom of a narrow staircase with closed doors to either side.

He opened the door to the left to reveal a small sitting-room, minimally furnished with a suite and a small, low table. The sunlight streamed in pleasantly enough through the two small windows highlighting the lacklustre wallpaper and the sombre nature of the fireplace. He closed the door with some degree of dubious satisfaction.

The right-hand door led into a slightly larger living-room, which although sparsely furnished, had far greater appeal than the previous room. Such appeal, in fact, he was beginning to envisage himself staying there after all. It was the primitiveness and old-fashioned charm of this place that was urging him to change his mind. There was a one-armed *chaise longue* beneath the window and a white-scrubbed table in the centre with two ladder-back chairs propped against it; but it was the old cast-iron grate and its hanging black kettle that really caught his eye! It was very like one he'd seen before, belonging to an old Aunt - decades ago when he was a boy. He raised his eyes over the oaken mantelpiece and was drawn to the framed text with its ominous message:

PREPARE TO MEET THY GOD.

APRIL COTTAGE

Prepare to meet thy God? Not just yet, thank you!

Behind the curtained doorway, the poky scullery with its quarried floor and stone sink with single copper tap was just another rustic relic from the past, which filled him with nostalgia. Even though he'd only been a small child in the forties it all seemed so much a part of him. He thrust his head into the adjoining pantry to be rewarded with a port-hole-window glimpse of the huge water-tub in the back yard. Cheered by all of this and with boyish bravado, he wasted no time in mounting the narrow stairway to discover the two tiny bedrooms with their cosy dormer-windows and the cramped little bathroom with its sloping roof. Adequate towels and bed-linen were provided, but there was a slight musty smell pervading the atmosphere. He retreated downstairs and let in some fresh air via the open doorway.

Breathing in the mingled fragrances of the wild little garden, he stood shielding his eyes from the morning sun, instinctively aware that he was well and truly hooked. Those initial strange feelings of familiarity were now replaced with a sense of belonging. April Cottage felt right to him and he felt that he could happily spend the week here before the play moved down to London.

10

At four-o-clock, Guy was disturbed by the old-fashioned *tip and ring* noise of a telephone. He'd been so busy settling himself in that he'd completely failed to notice the whereabouts of the telephone, which was summoning him with an outdated, persistent peal. He followed the sound to the sitting-room, where he found it tucked below an armchair on what can only be described as an upturned box, varnished; presumably to look like a coffee table. He hurriedly scooped up the receiver to the unmistakably camp utterings of Oberon Mercer.

"For a moment, Guy love, I thought you hadn't arrived. I was just about to ring-off!"

"Sorry, 'Bron. Been having a game of hide-and-seek with the phone!"

Guy plunged himself into the badly sprung chair to find himself face-to-face with a decidedly dated television set.

"Just ringing to let you know the time of the tech. Three-thirty, tomorrow afternoon. Ronnie and I are getting ourselves organised; the *Godspell* amateurs have moved out, Thank the Almighty, and the house staff are busy clearing the stage before the set arrives early in the morning – and, Guy love, there's a great excitement here; everyone's winding themselves up for your arrival!" He rambled on despite Guy's usual groan. "One poor dear from front-of-house has a real thing for you – it seems she has a hot flush every time your name is mentioned! Lorna – that's her name; you'll have to steer clear of the box office, love, or she'll have you for breakfast!"

Oberon took Guy's silence as an indication for a subject-change.

"Now then, how are you settling in? No, don't tell me – let me picture it – a little white-washed cottage, chintzy curtains at the windows, a cosy armchair by the telly and all the fragrance of old musk! Correct?"

"Close!" Guy quipped. "The white paint's peeling, the springs on this particular chair have gone and by the look of this telly it could be on the blink! As for the fragrance of old musk – it's more a pong of old must!"

"Do you mean *must*, as in damp?"

"Indeed so!"

"Well you simply cannot stay there! You'll get a chill, Guy love! Now come back to the room here at the hotel – I'll make all of the arrangements!"

"Did you ever camp-out, 'Bron? Oh sorry, no offence, let me rephrase that. Did you ever do out-of-bounds and all that stuff?"

"Not likely, I like comfort and luxury too much, dear."

"Exactly! And I like testing myself in extreme conditions – as you should well know. So please let's have none of this 'come back to the hotel' malarkey. I want to get a bit of the *real* life, that's all.

"In a paint-peeling, musty old cottage?"

"Yes, and it's bloody marvellous! You can stick your five-star!"

"Oh well, please yourself!" Oberon retorted with gay abandonment. "Now, do you know your way back to the theatre?"

"No." Guy said vaguely, more interested in trying to discern the make of the television set.

"It's in the centre of Hanley."

"What is?"

"The theatre!" Oberon pleaded, with increasing frustration. "Follow the signs for Hanley, it's the city-centre of Stoke-on-Trent. The Theatre Royal is just off Piccadilly."

"Piccadilly? You'll be telling me they've got a Trafalgar-square next, complete with fountains!"

"No, but they've got a Fountain square without fountains! *Alright, Ronnie love – don't get your knickers in a twist, I'm coming!* Must go, Guy love, I'm needed in the wings. See you tomorrow if you haven't died of pneumonia. When I've rung-off, promise me you'll turn the heating up!"

"I'll have a job - there isn't any."

"What!? No central heating? You'll catch your death of cold!"

"Not with a real coal and log fire blazing away, 'Bron! And a kettle simmering away on the hob. Just off to make a nice hot cup of English tea now. Thanks for ringing and don't work too hard."

Guy had replaced the receiver before Oberon had a chance to reply, and in doing so, he had leaned closer towards the television set and could now make out the name *Ferguson* emblazoned on its logo.

"Right, Fergie, let's see if we can get a bit of life out of you."

Guy disconnected the plug and carried the whole thing through to the warmth of the other room where he spent the next half-hour fiddling with the tuners, until he was rewarded with a few grey images on the screen.

To say the room was a bit of a mess was an understatement. He'd fetched everything from the car and dumped them wherever they fell. A supply of groceries, brought up from his London apartment were spilling out of bags onto the scrub-top table with a couple of bottles of Beaujolais propping them up. A few stray tomatoes had rolled onto the quarried floor where the rest of his belongings were in disarray. Two buckets of coal were standing in front of the glowing grate with its little brass fender, whilst a pile of bark-shedding logs had littered the entire hearth-mat with debris. He'd spent most of the afternoon happily following the list of instructions, which he'd soon spotted on the back of the scullery door; the usual things like the whereabouts of the keys, the availability of electricity and water supplies; both primitive, yet so refreshingly pleasing to him. He'd given prime-time to the exquisite experience of getting a fire roaring in the old grate and watching the flickering glow of it lifting new life into the room.

Adventurously, like a boy-scout he'd been out collecting sticks from beneath the trees at the rear of the cottage, deliriously ignoring the instructions, which had suggested using firelighters from beneath the kitchen sink. The labelled key hanging from the rusty nail in the pantry had led him to the padlocked coal-house, where he'd found a hidden hoard of gleaming black nuggets and a pile of neatly cut logs.

11

At around nine-thirty that evening, persistent ringing hollered once again from the sitting-room. *I'm going to strangle whoever-this-is, ringing me at this time of night* Guy thought, reluctantly pulling himself up from the sofa, which he'd now moved into prime position in front of the range. He'd blissfully settled himself down with a glass of Beaujolais and was enjoying it with a cheese sandwich and the wondrous aroma of a crackling log fire.

Guy scooped up the receiver. "Yes?"

"Guy, is that you?"

Dear God! It's Dee! Anderson thought. "I'm afraid the master is out, currently." He said, adopting the drawl of a butler he'd once played.

"Guy, stop fooling about!"

"Who shall I say had called?" Guy continued the charade.

"You know damned well who's calling! I've been talking to Oberon and I'm very worried about you!"

"Well I wish you'd concern yourself with someone else for a change." He snapped, allowing his natural tone to shine back through.

"Don't be so bloody rude, Guy!"

"Well I'd just settled for the night…"

"You can't be in bed already!"

"No, but you've brought me from a very warm spot to a room that's like a morgue!"

"And that's precisely why I'm ringing; from what Oberon tells me, that place isn't fit to live in! We're both equally concerned about you. We can't risk you getting a chill; and that's what will happen if you sleep in a damp, unheated cottage. Think of the tour if nothing else! We both think you should be sensible and come back to the hotel."

"Do you?" He said, provokingly.

"I'm only thinking about you, Guy."

"I'm touched by your concern, Dee darling, but let me assure you, I won't be catching a chill. I'm as snug as the proverbial rug; at least I *was*!"

"So, you're admitting you're cold?"

"Yes! In this room! Where the phone happens to be! Not in the room where I was just relaxing with a drink and a spot of supper, in front of a splendid open fire to which I would dearly love to return; if you'll allow me?"

"Oberon says the place is damp!"

"Not damp, merely a little musty because it's probably been shut up for a while."

"It sounds revolting!"

"You wouldn't say that if you were here!" Words he immediately regretted.

"Let me be the judge of that. How do I get there?"

"You don't!"

"Why not?"

"Dee! I don't have to explain, do I? When will it sink in, Dee? I want to be alone!"

"Famous last words." She said resignedly.

"Yes, famous last words."

There was an uncomfortable silence. Guy could sense Dee's frustration through her heavy, sulking breaths into the receiver.

"I'll see you tomorrow then, Guy. At the theatre." She surrendered.

"Of course. And Dee, thank you."

"For what? Annoying you?"

"No – for thinking about me."

"I wish I could stop thinking about you."

"No, don't do that. I like you to think about me."

"You could have fooled me!"

"What's that perfume you're wearing?"

"What!?"

"It's quite lovely!"

"Are you trying to be funny?"

"No – it's very – *nice...*" His words trailed off as he now realised the heady whiff of perfume was pervading the room.

"Just how much have you been drinking, Guy? Too much by the sound of it! You'll finish up like Henry if you go on like that! He took me to a Chinese restaurant tonight and spent an obscene amount of money on booze. I've left him propping up the bar downstairs."

"Good old Henry" Guy muttered, now totally distracted by the fragrance surrounding him.

"The rest of them are out celebrating. I'm here in my lonely room, and you, the unreachable star, are there! And so – goodnight, Guy darling."

"Goodnight, Dee. See you tomorrow afternoon."

Guy dropped the receiver as a strange dizziness swept over him. He made his was back towards the fire. As he left the coldness of the sitting-room, the perfume followed him lingeringly; and for some unearthly reason, he was reminded of a deep-blue, old-fashioned scent-bottle labelled 'Evening in Paris'.

12

The dawn chorus should have been a thousand times more pleasant than those rattling trains of the previous morning; but nature's harmonious alarm-call was annoyingly ill-timed as far as Guy was concerned. Bleary-eyed and disorientated, he squinted at his watch and eventually concluded that it was far too early to rise on a Sunday morning!

Turning over with a groan he attempted to fall back to sleep but the continual chirruping and whistling made it impossible. Agitatedly thumping his frustration out onto the pillow, he rolled resignedly onto his back and frowned disagreeably at the added intrusion of sunlight shafting in through the dormer-window. Slowly he reconciled himself to all of this; becoming contentedly submissive to the busy twittering and chattering going on under the eaves. The faded roses on the papered walls were a haven of rest for his eyes and for some strange reason the opening lines of a long-forgotten poem had returned to haunt his memory.

'I remember, I remember the house where I was born, the little window where the sun came peeping in at morn.' Except this wasn't the house where Guy had been born; he'd first seen the light of day in a room of immense proportions at the stately old vicarage out in the Gloucestershire countryside. Now for services rendered, his widowed father, the retired Reverend Christian Anderson lived in a humbler estate on the outskirts of the parish; the small house having been charitably reserved as a place of retirement for notable and worthy parishioners.

Boyhood at the old vicarage, with its acres of rambling grounds, had been a mixture of highs and lows for Guy Anderson. The highs were obvious; bringing many memories of carefree, adventure-packed day over fields and woodlands where the source of the Thames rises in the Cotswold hills on its illustrious path to London. The lows were less obvious to those who had not been saddled with the handicap of being the only son of a parson. The disadvantages of this had been enough when he was a young boy, but it was in adolescence that he'd suffered most.

His parents had abhorred his ambitious whims to be an actor, and yet it was they who had started it all with their pressure, insisting that he should take an active part in all those amateur dramatic productions, which had been the

APRIL COTTAGE

mainstay of church funds. It had taken years of challenging work to prove to his mother and father that he had chosen the right profession, but in that time, particularly after his much-advertised, showbiz wedding, the rift had widened and he had seen little of either of them.

It was at his mother's funeral, seven years ago, accompanied by his wife, that he'd dutifully returned to the tiny Cotswold village, and it was on that very day that the long, harrowing estrangement between he and his father had finally been brought to an end.

"Your mother was always proud of you. Really proud!" the old gent had assured him as they'd clutched hands before parting once more. "And she wanted you to know that!"

Guy's remorse in having failed to visit his parents was profound. And consequently, he'd assured his father that his visits were now going to be much more frequent.

"Come when you can, m'boy! You'll always be welcome here, both of you."

With Roxanne clinging impatiently to his arm in the most insensitive manner, Guy had left the small Cotswold-stone house to return to the vastness of New York. The sight of his ageing father, feebly waving a hand as he'd stood alone at the little front-door had stayed with him ever since. After that, he'd called to see him whenever time had permitted, and he would be calling again at the end of the week on his way down to London.

Whilst vaguely trying to decipher the black-framed picture on the bedroom-wall, Guy was trying to imagine what kind of disturbing effect all the recent, vulgar publicity may be having on his father. Remote, as the Reverend Christian Anderson was from the ruthless gossips of this world, he could have hardly failed to have missed it.
Guy followed the shadows on the ceiling, idly reflecting on his father's name, which had always been a bit of an embarrassment to the old boy himself. *Fitting enough for a man of the cloth to be named 'Christian', but coupled with 'Anderson'? It does have more than a fairy-tale ring about it!* Guy presumed that his grandparents, of whom he knew little, must have had a sense of humour, or an uncanny vision of their son's future; though his father had always maintained that they had been thus inspired by the Pilgrim's Progress hero who made his way to the Celestial City. Guy then began wondering which hero, if any, could have been the inspiration behind his own Christian name: *Guy of Warwick, perhaps? Or Scott's Guy Mannering? Guy de Maupassant? What about Dam-buster Guy Gibson, now there was a chap! Guy Fawkes? ...Heaven forbids!* Guy mused on,

now almost immune to the dawn-chorus. *One would have expected pops to have insisted on a biblical name for his only son – like Jeremiah, or Elijah. Abraham Anderson? Moses Anderson? Jacob Anderson?* He stretched out to his full-length on the oak-framed bed. *Thank the Lord they'd settled for Guy!*

13

Not for the first time his eyes were drawn to the bedraggled curtained affair in the corner of the room. The tatty, beige-coloured drapes hung from wooden rings on a thick pole, which had been fixed across the angle of the corner. It was, he presumed, supposed to be some kind of makeshift wardrobe. *Must have been there for years,* he thought to himself, half-expecting the curtains to open with the emergence of a stringed puppet.

For some unaccountable reason, that corner-area of the room began to give Guy a most uncomfortable feeling, to the point where he had no option but to withdraw his stare and focus instead on the foot of the bed, where the incoming sunshine had settled its ring of white light. Drowsily he closed his eyes and listened to the continuing sounds from his feathered friends in the rafters. Then again, with a strange inner compulsion, he was staring through the creviced eyelids at that particular feature of the room, which he was now trying desperately to avoid.

In a sudden, crystallising moment, it all came flooding back to him. Last night he had lain gazing across at it through a haze of shaded moonlight. Half-mesmerised by the tantalising waft of the lingering perfume, the potency of which had induced a trance-like sleep, such that he had never known. From the realms of his mind he began to piece together the dream that had followed and discovered that the curtained-wardrobe had been paramount to it. Outlined in that corner of the room, the dream had presented him with the most desirable vision of a young woman – slender, with light-blonde hair falling to her shoulders, where dainty lace straps supported a sleek, white under slip. It was pleasant to recall how the clinging silk had glossed down over the curves of her body to the edging of the coffee-coloured lace at her lower thigh. He had no recollection of her face; it seemed his attention must have been drawn to the straight, dark seams skimming down her shapely legs, with the suggestive hint of a black suspender showing beneath the under slip.

He'd watched as she'd drawn back the railed curtain to take a pretty, yet decidedly dated, flowered frock from one of the hooks. She'd held it against her and gone towards the window where an oak-framed cheval mirror had stood. He failed to remember what happened beyond this, but indulged in the fascination of what he'd been able to recall. There was no cheval mirror by the window now, but the curtained-wardrobe, weirdly drab in the early dawn-light, remained like some hallowed shrine; and disturbingly so. So disturbingly, that Guy found himself rising from the bed to get dressed, battling against the curious desire to continue staring in that direction.

14

Blast the technical rehearsal, it's not even necessary! Sod it all, we know the thing inside out! Guy had uselessly protested to himself from the moment he'd left the cottage that afternoon. It was the mere aggravation of having to tear himself away from the unique tranquillity of April Cottage, with its unexplored idyllic surroundings and consequently, his disgruntled departure had been left until the very last minute.

On reaching Hanley's town-centre, he ventured unflinchingly down a couple of deserted streets, clearly signposted for buses only, before finally finding himself on the unimpressive Piccadilly, with its empty pavements and Sabbath-closed stores. He knew he was now in the immediate vicinity of the Theatre Royal and therefore was scanning up and down the side-streets, where several of the play's familiar posters were daubed over various shop doorways. Before long, he saw Oberon's yellow Beetle parked on yellow lines alongside Dee's Mini, right outside the steps of the theatre. There was a prohibited space left for *his* car too.

"Guy love, you've made it!" came a call from the wings.

"Where in God's name have you been?" Dee demanded, descending from stage to auditorium to meet him in the central gangway. "We're waiting to get on with it!"

"Let's get on with it then" said Guy, nonchalantly brushing her aside in order to see the stage from front-of-house.

There it was again. That hideous floral settee at centre, and the teak coffee table with the red telephone, and same old pile of boxed, artificial hydrangeas still blooming by the open French-windows, and the mock statuette on the patio beyond where the horrendous murder of the elderly Ezra Jackson predictably took place every evening.

Old Henry was there on the set, already ensconced into his wicker chair for the short, but vital role of the unfortunate Ezra, and now casting a welcoming glance in Guy's direction.

"Good!" He proclaimed. "We can finally make a start now that you've arrived. I've got a pain in my back-side with sitting on this thing!"

"Don't worry Henry, we'll soon have you face down on the patio again." Guy's assurance was echoed up into the gods.

Producer Violet, whose every word was sacred, appeared to give a final briefing before leaving for her countless other commitments in London.

"Okay Everyone, on stage please!" She demanded. "I'd like a word before we begin – just a few slight technical problems to iron-out and then it should all be plain sailing!"

To Guy's relief, they managed to skip large amounts of the script and by six-o-clock everyone was leaving the building.

"What do you think of the place?" Oberon asked as they approached their cars respectively.

Guy looked up at the exterior of the theatre. "I have to admit it, 'Bron, I've seen worse than this in the West-end."

"They tell me that it was built in nineteen-fifty-one; shortly after the *old* Theatre Royal went up in flames, with the costumes and scenery of the Sadler's Wells Ballet Company who, poor dears, happened to be doing a week's run here. Apparently, all went well here after the new theatre was built with a good run of shows and celebrities; but then the cash ran out! For several years this place was dark and the dreaded Bingo-boys moved in. Live theatre was resumed thanks to a band of local theatre-lovers who pulled out all the stops to make it what it is today, and what's more; I believe it's all been done on a shoe string."

"Then good luck to 'em!" Guy said, sprawling into the driving seat and fixing his seat belt.

"Guy love, why don't you join us at the hotel for dinner before you go?" Oberon called invitingly over the door of his Beetle.

"Yes, why don't you?" added a breathless Delia who'd made a frantic dive to meet him before he left.

"Sorry, I've got things to do." Guy said decisively, closing the car door.

"What *things?*" she asked, purposefully leaning into the car to prevent him from closing the window.

"Things!"

"Well I want to come and help you with these – err, *things*!"

Her face was close enough for him to feel the menthol-scented warmth of her breath on his mouth. He stared into the mascara-lashed green eyes so effectively appealing to him through her square-framed glasses and for the briefest of moments, he weakened.

"Please try to understand, Dee darling."

"What is there to understand about someone who wants to be alone in some grotty little cottage?" Her hair brushed against his face. "Can't you see I'm concerned about you, Guy?"

"Don't be, I enjoy the primitive way of life."

"Me too - so let's go and be very *primitive* together, shall we?"

"Sorry Dee, but I prefer the solitude that goes with it." He removed her straying hand from his knee. "…So, you go back to your palatial hotel, have dinner and a nice civilised Sunday-evening with the rest of them, and I'll see you for the opener tomorrow night, okay? Come on, give me a peck on the cheek to show there're no hard feelings?"

The peck on the cheek was delivered quickly, and was fast developing into a mouth-watering delicacy of a kiss, which might have had more than his taste buds going if it hadn't been for two pairs of searching hands thrusting autograph books in through the car window. The outraged Dee turned to face two female predators, all hot breath and heaving bosoms, remorselessly intent on forcing themselves in, and her out.

"Well, Guy, if it's the primitive way of life you want – there's a prize pair of primates right here – so I'll leave you to them!" she stormed off, into her car.

After appeasing his admirers by hurriedly scrawling his name out a couple of times, he thrust his head out of the window in time to see the black-topped Mini hurtling dangerously out-of-sight."

15

A single church bell was ringing as he passed through the hamlet on his return to the cottage, summoning what could have only been a handful of people to Evensong. Summoning was the word if the horrendous clang of that bell was anything to go by; it sounded more like someone hitting a dustbin lid. Guy knew quite a bit about bells; when he was young he'd spent many an hour in the belfry of his father's church, curiously observing the concentrated effort on the rigid faces of that circle of stalwarts who'd attended weekly bell practice with such undaunted regularity.

His car moved swiftly and silently away from the hamlet, up and along the tree-lined slope soon passing the white-walls of the farm house. The ominous, almost absurd clanging of that distant bell now diminished into obscurity, leaving him with a sudden, unaccountable sense of loss, tempered by a transient sepulchral tolling in the ears. He almost felt like some erstwhile Dick Whittington – *turn again Anderson – return again Anderson* – return to what?

The unanswered thought drifted from his mind as he was again struck by the familiarity of the scene now confronting him. The wooded hillside road, now descending and curbing into the bend where the crumbling grey wall met the narrow lane's no-thoroughfare sign, and there just yards ahead of him was the small hanging gate and the five stone steps of April Cottage. All other emotions were surpassed by the inherent, deep-seated sense of belonging, and the enigma of why it should be so.

He had vague recollections of hearing about other people finding themselves in strange surroundings with a strong feeling of having been there before; but this was the first time it had ever happened to the widely-travelled Guy Anderson.

16

The embers in the kitchen-room grate needed no more than a poke to set them aflame. With the addition of a log and a few lumps of coal the hearth was aglow and the old iron kettle was soon singing on the hob. Guy fetched in tomatoes and cheese from the scullery and placed them on the table with a loaf of bread, butter and pickles. In no time at all he had a pot of tea made and a well-filled sandwich on his plate.

He sat at the table staring into the firelight and was uniquely and utterly at peace with himself. He'd never been one for dwelling on the complexities on the meaning of life, but here, in April Cottage, the sheer simplicity of everything was magical; here he could see, with such clarity of vision, the whole lousy imposture of his so-called public-image.

The sandwich was wholesome and delicious; just enough salt on the tomatoes, a dash of pungent chutney, and a generous slice of mature cheddar on the crusty bread. This plain English ploughman-supper was ambrosia supreme and, he mused, far superior to any of Roxanne's bean-feasts. He tried not to recall her volatile table-offerings which, apart from the odd taco and lettuce-leaf, had been 'hot' everything: *hot-peppered, hot-dogged*; not only that but she was *hot-headed* and *hot-bedded* into the bargain. He took another hefty bite at the sandwich.

After clearing away the dinner things he felt like a stroll and reckoned it was still light enough to venture up the lane. He set off at that unreal moment in time when the gently dipping sun has cast its magenta glow over everything in sight. The hawthorn-blossomed hedgerows sprawled contemptuously over both sides of the lane, which was no more than a track with a rough surface of hardened gravel. He wondered how far this no-through road would take him before it came to an abrupt end. *What then?* Perhaps a five-barred gate to a field with a keep-out notice or 'Beware of the Bull!'

Whatever lay further on up this road, Guy was getting a feeling that another cottage was going to appear along the way somewhere. That strange sense of familiarity was creeping in again as his mind conjured up a lone dwelling-place with pebble-dashed walls. *Surely such a presumptive premonition was about to be pebble-dashed!* Undeterred he strode on with all the inquisitiveness of an intrepid explorer.

APRIL COTTAGE

The track ahead was straight for about a quarter of a mile before veering at right-angles into the direction of a blinding sunset. With the full strength of it forcing him to shield his eyes, Guy could see that he'd reached the end of the lane, and what lay ahead forced a sharp intake of breath.

"Now, that's weird!" he whispered to himself as his feet shuddered to a halt. There, silhouetted against the blood-orange sky, was a small house with pebble-dashed walls, exactly as he'd foreseen moments ago. Very slowly, he moved closer to the dingy, grey building. Shadowed against the fading light of the sky it stood as silent as the grave and he wondered who on Earth could possibly be living there. There was no light at the drawn-curtained windows; no car in sight and not the slightest sound or movement in place. The morbid thought occurred to him that if someone had been lying dead in there – no-one would be any the wiser; and at that time of night, he wasn't prepared to find out! *In any case,* he bargained with himself, *it may be the home of some infirm old lady who would be scared out of her wits by a dusk-time stranger knocking at her door!*

Guy peered through a gap in the hedge, getting a glimpse of a rusty old bike leaning against a shack of a shed. He was about to turn when something moved in the holly bush beside him. He looked down to see a hostile, snarling feline hissing at him from within a circle of dead leaves. It was a long-haired cat with piercing tiger-like eyes, open-clawed and menacingly about to spring. He didn't know who was more scared – *him or the cat* – but due to his recent eerie experiences, coupled with the ever-darkening dusky atmosphere slowly depriving him of his sight, Guy had viewed this cat as a portent and within seconds he was back on the lane towards April Cottage.

17

Later in the evening there was a nonsensical play on the television's only usable channel, with an intermittent roll on the screen, which didn't help for viewing. Mouthing the word 'tripe!' he switched off, reaching for the newspaper and flicking through the pages. He soon tossed it aside to yawn into the firelight with the prospect of basking there, in pensive mood, before retiring. Before long, he found himself recalling his premonition of the pebble-dashed cottage – *it had to be coincidence, of course! Or perhaps a quirk of the imagination?* But then, he conjectured, *somewhere in the dim and distant past, I might have been here before. Perhaps when I was a child?* Deciding that he would be able to consult his father on that matter, he drank the last drop of red wine and sprawled back, haphazardly into the cushions on the *chaise-longue*. He closed his eyes feeling the wonderful warmth of the fire on his face, and drowsily inhaled the narcotic smell of burning bark as it crackled away into charcoal. The neatly clipped moustache lifted at the corners of his mouth where a fixed smile of contentment had lazily established itself.

The drifting twilight sleep that followed was soon to be shrivelled out of existence by the sudden onset of inconsolable, grief-stricken sobbing, which remorselessly invaded the channels of his ears until he was sitting bolt upright and cursing the mature cheddar. He stared into the last remnants of burned-out wood striving to shake-off his slumber's disturbing tale of a maiden-in-distress. Now awake and alert, he craved for silence, but the anguished cries lingered on in his brain. *What in Heaven's name am I hearing? How am I still hearing it? There it is again...Dear God, this is no dream!*

The distressing sounds were coming from somewhere in the house!

18

He could hear it more clearly now. The plaintive sounds led him to the closed door of the sitting-room. Bewildered and disorientated he stood there listening, half-afraid to intrude. The crying was now reduced to a whimper as though she, whoever she was, was aware of his approach. Totally in awe of what he might see he opened the door rather gently and reached for the light switch, but there was nothing. Nothing to see and nothing to hear. Nothing at all. Just a cold, empty room with stunning silence.

Guy stood still for a while, feeling a warm rush of blood to his face as a wave of fear washed over him. Suddenly, it seemed that some strange feminine force was leading him, imploringly and beseechingly, into the centre of the room where he stood hovering, zombie-like; until the prickling hairs on the back of his head sent the goose bumps rippling down his spine. Mercifully released from the force that had held him, he left the room with the same intrusive steps one would take when leaving a chapel of rest.

"Dear God!" he spoke aloud, mounting the stairs two at a time.

Eventually enveloped within the sanctity of the sheets, he lay still until the ultimate warmth began to calm his trembling limbs. His only reassurance was the bedside lamp, comfortingly illuminating the black-framed picture on the rose-patterned walls as he lay pondering on the very real possibility of this cottage being haunted; a thought that was alien to everything he had previously believed in – but then he came to the far more acceptable fact that this brief sojourn on the sofa must have lengthened into a continuing dream, which had merely *seemed* like reality; and it was almost certain, as he'd initially thought, that Beaujolais and mature cheddar had been the main culprits.

With some degree of satisfaction, he turned over, pulling the sheets around him – but then his eyes were drawn to the curtained wardrobe once again. He closed his eyes to avoid it. If sleep ever came that night, Guy thought hopefully, it would be quite desirable to dream of that flowery-frocked blonde in the silk stockings!

19

The ensuing sleep was dreamless; even sublime, and by early morning light it had distanced Guy from the morbidity of his wild imaginings – preparing him to rise and face normality. Everything else seemed normal enough as he dutifully scanned over his script whilst waiting for the kettle to boil. After slowly savouring that first cup of tea he gleefully speared a thick round of bread and toasted it over the open fire. Toast had never tasted better, and still crunching one round he commenced to toast another with the makeshift toasting fork. The heat from the fire radiated onto his face as he leaned to get a nostalgic whiff of the charring chunk of crusty bread.

This unique moment of divinity was soon to be violated by an urgent sharp rapping at the window. Guy turned to see an ungainly shape blotting out the daylight with a huge face pressed into horrific distortion against the panes. The toast dropped into the fire and in trying to retrieve it, Guy flinched in pain as his fingers caught the heat of the short metal fork. Still wincing in pain, he left the burning effigy in the fire to face the grinning effigy at the window.

"Who's there?" he snarled, glaring at the hulk in an anorak and woollen hat. "You do realise this is private property?".

"You'll have to move your car, mister!" the muffled voice urged against the panes.

"What!?"

"I can't get past with me truck, right?"

"I can't hear what you're saying?"

"Yer car's blockin' me way, right? I can't get past with me truck, right?

Guy opened the window with more than a little irreverence. "Look here! What do you think you're doing gaping into the room like that? Haven't you heard of knocking at the door?"

"I saw you through the window, mister! So I tapped, right?" the man grinned, revealing a row of rotten teeth.

"Wrong!" Guy snapped. "You nearly shattered the glass! And thanks to you, I've burned myself! What the hell are you doing snooping around here at this time of the morning?"

"Snooping!?" he obviously took great exception to the accusation. "I'm not snooping, mister, I'm not!"

"Well, what *are* you doing?"

"Deliverin' the milk, right?"

"I don't want any milk!"

"Maybe you don't, mister! But there's them that do! Old George lives down the lane at Holly Cottage. He wants milk! I bring him a crate of it every Monday morning. Got a lot of cats has George. But y'see, mister, there's no way I can get past that car of yours with me truck. If y'can just move it a touch, I'll be able to get through, right?"

Guy stared at the grinning face with growing impatience. "Just a minute, I'll get my keys" he said, full of resentment as he went in search of his briefcase.

"You staying 'ere long, mister? The man asked, warily projecting his upper half through the open window and casting furtive glances around the room.

"That's none of your business!" Guy snapped, returning with the keys.

"They don't stay 'ere long. None of 'em! And I knows why! I knows why they don't stay long!" he chortled until his features contorted into a hideous mass of purple pulp. "It's because of *her*! It's *her* who always drives 'em away. I knows it!"

"What the devil are you talking about now, man?"

"I take it you've not heard anything then, mister?"

"Heard what?" Guy asked, trying to conceal his mounting unease.

"The wailing ghost woman!" The answer was provided with all the relish of a fiendish oaf at a funeral.

"Don't talk such bloody rubbish, man!" Guy said avoiding the piggy little eyes by going to the front door. He strode off down the garden path whilst muttering to himself about the poor sod being on day release from a nearby insane asylum. The man shuffled close on his heels.

Guy descended the five stones steps very thoughtfully. No matter what his opinion of this man was; he had undoubtedly touched a nerve. As they reached the car he turned to face him. "What did you mean by all that rubbish?"

The man's bloated face bulged into a victorious grin. "By all that rubbish, mister?"

"You know damned well! All that stuff about…"

"Oh, you mean that wailing ghost woman?" he asked provocatively. Guy waited for him to go on. "Well, they do say…" he lingered on these words, speaking far slower now with a darker tone in a childish attempt to create a spooky and suspenseful atmosphere. Guy, with his lifetime of theatrical experience, was becoming more impatient by the second.

"What do they say!? Come on, man! – out with it! What do they say?

"*They* say…they say that close on midnight, right? …Close on midnight, you can hear the wailing of the ghost woman!"

"Wailing?" Guy asked derisively, "What do you mean, *wailing*?"

"Y'know, mister! Wailing! Like crying! Cries her eyes out *they* say! I reckon that's why this place is shuttered up for weeks on end. It belongs to the estate, y'know, like Holly Cottage down the lane; which reminds me – I must get down there. Old George *dunna* like his cats getting 'ungry!"

"Does George live in the pebble-dashed house at the end of the lane?"

"There's only one house down there, right - so, I reckon he does. He's lived up there all his life and he must be close on eighty! He's a queer old stick is George!"

Takes one to know one, Guy thought to himself as he clambered into his car.

Seconds later, the battered old milk truck was slowly shuddering the ground as it inched its way alongside the blue Jaguar. Guy remained seated at the wheel, watching until the back of the truck dwindled on into the hidden depths of the lane. Having remained there for a considerable amount of time, deep in thought, the truck was already making its cumbersome return as Guy remounted the steps. He paused, looking down on the clattering assembly of crated bottles re-shunting against the cart, and he continued to watch until the vibrating hulk of a vehicle had rolled out of sight.

The awful slob of a man was driving away doltishly, oblivious of the quandary he'd left behind. His bigoted bantering of the wailing ghost woman had been a crude vindication of something Guy had so readily cast aside as being nothing more than the hallucinating, dreamy effects of undigested cheese and wine.

With measured steps, he returned towards the mellowing walls of the cottage and the foreboding enticement of the half-opened doorway. Stopping by the apple-tree he nervously fingered the ridges on the bark as he was now vowing to make a hasty departure. Above him, the pink and white blossom was riveted with shimmering blades of morning sunlight and as he gazed upwards through the spectrum, searching for some kind of reassuring sign. Somewhere above the straying clouds an aeroplane droned, blissfully remote; Guy felt a strange kind of mystical empathy with whoever was piloting that plane, fully realising the sheer exhilaration of flying through the magnitude of space; exalted above all earthly things.

    Somewhat consoled and gratified by this transient diversion he eventually went back inside and poured himself a comforting drink from the teapot on the hob, but was unable to avoid the nagging question of whether or not he should be packing his bags. According to that fool of a milkman, the place was haunted and last night's little episode in the sitting-room would seem to substantiate his claim.

20

There has to be some foundation! Some reason! Some explanation for what he'd heard in the sitting-room. Some explanation for the total subjection that had encompassed him when he had gone in there to investigate. Some explanation for the chilling fear and trepidation that had forced him out.

Glancing around the sunlit kitchen, such fears seemed very remote. He felt cocooned by the rustic walls and the timelessness of the place. He felt that he belonged there. Why then, should he allow fear and ignorance to drive him out? Someone somewhere must know something that would explain the reason for those tragic sounds of a woman sobbing in distress. He had to know more. *Much more!*

The opportunity for finding out came much quicker than he could have anticipated.

21

Standing by the bedroom window, pulling a cashmere sweater over his head, Guy saw someone strolling down on the lane. Like a shot, he was down the stairs, through the door and at the end of the garden path. As he leaned over the gate, the tall, elderly man was moving at a snail's pace towards him.

"Good morning there!" Guy hollered.

The man lurched to a halt, raising his eyes through thick lenses beneath the brim of a battered cap.

"Nice morning?" Guy mused towards the man, smiling very genially. "I'm staying here for a short while – just a few days that is. Are you from the other cottage down there?"

"What's that to you?" the man demanded, with a lined old face, full of suspicion.

"As we seem to be neighbours, I just figured that I should make myself known to you, sir, that's all."

"Aye!" he muttered guardedly, "but I think I should be getting back now."

"Very pleasant around here; particularly at this time of year!" Guy continued hurriedly, despite the man's reluctance to communicate. "I don't expect you see many people around here?"

"No" the man turned himself slowly around to inch his way back down the lane.

"Hold on a moment!" Guy urged, as he descended the steps to the lane with the man shuffling on regardless. "Please don't go for a minute; you see, I was wondering if you could help me? I believe your name is George, am I right?"

The man stopped with a reproachful grimace. "How would you know that?"

"The milkman told me…"

"He has too much to say, that one! Needs to mind his own business!"

"Yes, I agree with you. He told me one or two things, which quite frankly have disturbed me." Guy noticed an expression of concern creep over the old man's face. "Oh, nothing about you, George, I can assure you – it was more to do with this place; April Cottage. If you don't mind, I'd like to ask you a few questions about it?"

"It's no good asking me, sir! I know nothing about anything! I just keep myself to myself and that's the way I like it."

Guy couldn't help but allow a wry smile to appear in the corner of his mouth. "That's the way

I like it too, George. I think you and I have a lot in common!"

"I don't think so, sir."

"But we have, George, we have!" Guy continued, encouragingly. "I hope you don't mind me calling you George."

"Why should I? It's me name!"

"A mighty-fine name too!" Guy remarked, hoping it didn't sound too patronising. "Look, George, all I need is a little help from you, and nothing more."

"Help? No, I'm sorry, sir; I don't do any jobbing these days. No, I'm past all that now – it takes all my time to keep Holly Cottage going. You can get some help from yonder at the farm; there's a family of young 'uns – though I doubt there's much work in any of 'em. So, Good-day to you, sir." He touched his battered old cap and turned away.

Guy called after him. "I don't mean that kind of help, George! I just want to make a few enquiries."

The man stopped abruptly. "I knew it!" he snapped. "I knew it as soon as I clapped eyes on you!"

"Knew what, George?"

"You're with the law, aren't you!?" he barked accusingly with his pin-point eyes peering through the thick lenses of his spectacles.

"I'm not with the law! You've been watching too much television, George!" Guy grinned, assuming the old gent must have seen the famous inspector series he'd done for the independent network.

"Television, sir? I wouldn't have one in the place!"

"Then you're a wise man, George. Now how about coming to have a nice cup of tea with me before you head back to Holly Cottage? You'd like a good old *cuppa* and a little chat, wouldn't you, George?"

"I told you, sir, I'm nothing for chatting – and I can have a mug of tea when I get home. Thank you all the same, sir" he touched his cap again and turned to go.

"Well, what about a drop of good whiskey then?" Guy saw the sudden hesitancy in the old man's step. "I've got a nice, matured bottle of *Special Reserve*, if you'd care for a drop before you head back?"

"Whiskey?" the old man said, turning and retracing his steps. "*Special reserve*, you say? It seems you have good taste, and I was never one for turning down a drop of whiskey, sir!"

22

"No, George…please don't bother taking your boots off! Come on in and sit down by the fire…"

"Thank you, I'll enjoy a quick warm; it may be April but there's a bit of a nip in the air, and I do seem to feel the cold a bit more these days; the old blood's getting a bit thinner, you know!"

"This will get it going around your veins a bit quicker, George!" Guy was pouring a generous measure of whiskey into a glass as the old gent stood warming himself by the fire-grate.

"Do you like water with it? Guy asked.

"Water!?" he scoffed. "Why douse good scotch with water? Defeats the object, doesn't it?"

"Here we are then, George. Sit down and make yourself comfortable."

"I mustn't stop long, sir! It's me cats y'see…I'll just have a minute or two with you, then I'll be off back to them."

Guy held onto the drink until his guest had seated himself precariously on the edge of the sofa.

"I mustn't mess up your nice seat, sir. I've got me old rabbiting coat on. It's seen a fair few winters has this old coat – just like its owner!" His gnarled, shaking hand, clad in a fingerless glove, accepted the drink. "My word! This is a real treat for me, sir. I haven't had a drop of scotch for years!"

"Years, George?"

"Aye, sir, years! Me old mother used to keep a drop in – for her chest, y'know? And we'd have a nip or two then. She's been dead and gone for some time now. The best I do for meself is brew up a bottle or two of ma' parsnip wine every now and again." He took a good sip of the whiskey and for the first time, he gave a broad, approving smile in Guy's direction. "My, that's grand, sir…grand! A real malt whiskey, that is! Aye!"

"So, now your mother's gone you live on your own, do you, George?"

"Alone? No, I'm not on me own, sir."

"Oh, you're married, are you?"

"Married? Ha! No woman'd have me, sir! And can you blame 'em? But I'm not on me own…far from it! I live with me cats – I've got ten of 'em!"

"Ten cats!?"

"Aye, ten old moggies – and I wouldn't be surprised if there isn't more when I get back. Flossie's in kindle again!"

"Flossie?"

"Aye...she's been at it again!" His face creased into a merry grin and he chuckled to himself as he sipped more whiskey. "I suspect Willie. It could be Charlie, but I suspect Willie. Fond of his *willie*, is our Willie!" Once again, the old man chuckled at his own attempt at humour. "He's the ginger – the dirty rascal caught her under the dresser – didn't half make her squawk!"

"Poor old Flossie" Guy mused.

"Not it! She enjoyed every minute of it!" he said, still chuckling and sipping at his drink. "But I'll wager a bet that old Willie enjoyed it more! A rare rascal, that one! Ginger-striped from head to tail and as sharp as a whisker, aye!"

"I'll have to pop down and meet your cats, George."

"You'd be welcome, sir!"

"And less of the *sir*, for goodness sake! Call me Guy"

"Call you what, sir?"

"Guy! That's my name! Now then, George..." Guy was desperately trying to turn the conversation around to the unanswered questions about the cottage. George must know something if he'd lived at Holly Cottage all his life, but he could see it wasn't going to be easy.

"Funny sort of name that, sir! Guy! We used to call out *'a penny for the Guy'* when we were nippers, right before we'd go and chuck him on the bonfire and watch him burn!"

Guy raised an eyebrow and felt slightly humoured by George's morbid reference. "Yes, George. I remember, in my schooling days, the ribbing I used to get with a name like Guy. It's Guy Anderson, by the way…" Guy waited to see if there was a reaction from George. He was relieved when there wasn't.

"My name's Smith. You can't get more common than that, can you? But I've got a right royal Christian name to go with it – aye! There's been a few George's on the English throne, y'know!"

"There has indeed! Now then, George, I wanted to ask you…"

"Aye! I've got a lot of respect for royalty myself! They do a lot of good for the old country of ours. Me old mother was fond of royalty too; she once saw Queen Mary in the flesh. I've never seen any of 'em…though once I came close enough to the late king in me army days. Aye, I was posted to a London barracks during the war. I've route-marched passed Buckingham Palace a few times, I can tell you!"

"Really?" Guy said a little wearily, trying to sound interested.

"Oh, yes!". There was a sudden burst of pride. "It's a grand place at close quarters, sir! Have you seen it?

"Many times, George…but then, I live in London most of the time"

"Then you'll know how grand it is, sir? They still have their dogs running around the place, do they?"

"Yes, the queen is very fond of her corgis!"

"She'd be better having cats! Keep the mice down for her in the palace! I never seen a single mouse down at Holly Cottage and that's a fact!

"So, if Her Majesty has any little unwanted visitors, George, you'll have to send Willie along to sort them out!" Guy said, stifling the urge to laugh.

"No, sir…I'd send our Nellie! She's the mouser! Sharp as a whisker she is! Old Willie is too busy doing *other things*, the dirty little rascal!" George raised the tumbler to his lips and swallowed the remainder of his beverage in one gulp. "Well, that was a lovely drop of whiskey, sir, but I'd best be off back to Holly Cottage now…and thank you kindly, sir, you're a scholar and *gent*!" He was about to rise, but Guy still hadn't got an atom of information out of the old man.

"Oh, come on, George, have one more for the road, here we are…"

"Well, as you're offering, sir; I won't say no to another little drop!"

"There we go..." Guy smiled, pouring another good measure and grinning to himself at the way the old man was thrusting out his glass. "Now then, George – I was hoping you may be able to give me a bit of information..."

"I doubt it, sir. I don't mind admitting that I've always been a bit of a duffer. Me old mother used to say that when they handed out brains, I was at the back of the queue!"

"I don't intend to pick your brains, George – just jog your memory a little, that's all – just simple things that you might remember; like the history of this place, for instance?"

"History!? What I know about history could go on a postage stamp, sir!" He chuckled into his whiskey tumbler.

"Not that kind of history, George...what I really want to know is something about the people who have lived here, at April Cottage, in the past?"

"Well it's no use asking me that either; I've never had any time for making acquaintances with folk. I prefer cats to people, I do. All I can tell you is that, these days, there's been many a stranger staying here and I've never as much as opened ma' mouth to any of 'em. That is until today, when you came and made a point of speaking to me. I don't make a habit of speaking to strangers. I like to mind ma' business!"

"I know, George – and I think that's very wise – but I'm not talking about people like me who come and rent this place for a week or two; I'm talking about the people who've actually lived here in the past. I thought you might know, having lived here for a very long time?"

"All ma' life, sir!"

"Well in that case, you must've known who was living here? Say, twenty years ago? Or perhaps thirty years ago? Or even as far back as the forties? Can you remember who was here in the forties, George?"

"Now you're asking me! I shall have to get ma' old thinking cap on! It's a funny thing, sir, but although I was born and bred in these parts, I don't remember much about folk – I've always been a bit of a loner, y'see! In fact, I'd go as far to say that I haven't set foot in this cottage since the Fosters were here back in the thirties!"

"The Fosters!?" Guy pounced on the name. "Yep, go on, George – tell me about the Fosters…"

"there isn't much too tell. I remember there were quite a family of 'em – and a rowdy lot of ruffians they were, too! We were glad when they'd all gone I can tell you!"

"Is that all you can tell me about them, George?"

"There's nowt else to tell – except that they were rough and rowdy! Nowt else about them that would interest a gentleman and scholar like yourself, sir."

"I try to be a gentleman, but I can assure you I'm no scholar!"

"I think you're a scholar, sir! You've got breeding and an educated voice!"

"That's only theatre-training, George. I work in the theatre."

"Theatre, eh? I've never been to a theatre in my life! Never been anywhere except when the war broke out! That was the only time when I was away from these parts. Like a fish out of water, I was! I suppose you don't remember much about the war, sir?"

"No, I was born during the war – nineteen forty-two to be precise."

"Nineteen forty-two! That takes me back to the army days. They were dark days then; we all had to put our backs into it!"

"Who was living here then, George, in the war years?"

"That's when we were striving for victory! Victory at all costs!"

"Who was in then, George?"

"Good old Winnie was in then!"

APRIL COTTAGE

"Winnie who? It's important, George!"

"Well if you don't know who Winnie was, you're a bigger duffer than I thought you were!" he retorted thunderously, whilst removing his cap and rising rather unsteadily to his feet. He raised a glass giving Guy a contemptuous glare. "Winnie won us the war! *'Never in the field of human conflict was so much owed by so many to so few!'* I thought everyone knew that?"

Guy tried to hide his impatience. "Oh, I'm sorry, George – I didn't realise you were referring to Sir Winston Churchill!" Guy was on his feet joining in as a remark of respect until the old boy had completed the quote. "I thought..."

"Now there was a true Englishman if ever there was one!" George interrupted, with reverence, replacing his cap and sitting down again.

Guy flopped down beside him on the sofa, exhausted and deflated by his inability to get anything out of this indomitable old fellow. It was clear he wasn't going to get any information regarding the cottage. Perhaps he should sit back and just enjoy the chat and the whiskey, as his newfound friend was doing.

"Aye! Old Winnie saw it through to the end, and I don't mind saying there was none gladder than me to get back to me mother and her apple pie! It was the only time that she and me had been parted, sir – and she missed me as much as I missed her! She was a good old soul, always busying herself with something! Did a lot of decent work herself when the war was on – aye! Did a lot of knitting for the forces – knit until her knuckles were sore – socks, scarves and balaclavas by the score! And right neighbourly she was too, in those dark days! Thinking back, she spent quite a bit of time within these very walls being neighbourly!"

Guy sat bolt upright. "Being neighbourly here? Here, George? Your mother came here in the forties? To this cottage?"

"Aye! Well it gave her something to do. Kept her out of mischief whilst I was away helping good old Winnie to win the war!"

"Yes, George, yes – but at that time, who was in then?"

"I'll tell you who was in then – ATTLEE!" He spat out the name with venom. "Winnie was out and Attlee was in! That's gratitude for you!"

Guy could do nothing but wait until the old soldier had regained his composure.

"Yes, I understand how you felt about that, but I meant who was in this cottage at that time, when your mother used to come and visit?"

George sipped at his whiskey and stared rather blankly around the room before continuing.

"It was a very sad affair, actually – and best forgotten about, sir."

"I'd like to know about it, George. Please tell me about it…"

"I can't think why, sir, but since you're asking, I'll tell you what bit I can remember. You see – on occasions, ma' mother would come up here and sit with the young wench during the blackout…"

"Young wench!?"

"Yes, she was living here then. She was left on her own; when her husband was in the forces, just like the rest of us. They hadn't been married long and they'd just bought this place and settled down as you might say. Ma' mother came helping out a bit, 'cause this young wench was expecting a baby y'see, sir…" He paused for a moment before gravely adding "then the unwelcome news came! That poor young fellow had been shot down over Germany!"

"The husband?"

"Aye, sir. Killed in action, he was! It was a tragedy. I remember ma' mother saying that there was no consoling that poor young widow. She cried and cried for days. There's those around here that say her cries *still* haunt this very cottage!"

23

Guy felt the hairs on the back of his neck bristling as he stared into the glowing fireplace. "What happened to her, George?"

"She died having the baby. That's what the midwife said – but ma' mother always said that she died of a broken heart, aye! I never clapped eyes on her m'self, but I remember ma' mother saying that when she came up here to lay her out, she was beautiful, even in death. Ma' mother, bless her, came and did all the arrangements; there was no-one else around to do them kind of things with everyone off to the war..."

"And the baby died too?"

"No – I think they saved the baby; there was talk of some kind of adoption." Guy sat in stunned silence as the old man pulled himself to his feet. "I told you it was best forgotten about, didn't I, sir? No sense in reaping up the past I say. Well I'd best be on my way to see how Flossie's getting on. Thank you kindly for the Scotch, sir – it was a real treat, aye!"

"George…" Guy followed him to the door. "Can you remember her name?"

"Now you're asking me something, sir! I've no memory for names!"

"Please try to remember, George" Guy urged, giving him a helping hand down the steps and seeing him safely onto the lane.

"Wait a minute, sir – I think I've got it! Aye, it was Mary, sir! That's it! Mary! I remember that whenever ma' mother used to talk about her, she used to hum that song. You probably won't remember it but it was very popular in the war days…*'For it was Mary, Mary long before the fashions came, but there was something there that sounds most rare, it's a grand old name'"*

After the tuneless rendition, he politely touched his cap and a little merrier for the drink, soldiered slowly on the homeward journey into the distance of the lane.

Guy went back into the cottage with the 'grand old name' hammering at his brain. Every nerve in his body was now acutely aware of Mary's existence; and in the precious few hours before this evening's performance, he was going to explore every avenue. Mary had now become more than a figment of the imagination! More than the effects of cheese and wine! More than a whiff of 'Evening in Paris' and much more than a dream!

APRIL COTTAGE

Mary had lived and breathed right here in April Cottage – and Mary had died here!

24

In the following hour, he took the car and drove to the little hamlet with its row of red-bricked cottages and tiny hillside churchyard; the latter being the object of his journey. There was no bell tolling now, just the silence of Monday's late afternoon. He moved slowly amongst the stone-shrouded mounds of the churchyard glancing down briefly over the rear view of the terraced cottages, each having an allotted span of walled garden where carefully cultivated lines of daffodils edged the minuscule squares of lawns.

It seemed that Guy was the sole inhabitant of this place as he picked his way through the long-grasses of the graveyard, now searching diligently and eagerly, trying to decipher the weatherworn inscriptions on countless tombstones. Several Mary's had been interred there but their sandstone epitaphs revealed that they were all of a long-forgotten era; eventually bringing him to the conclusion that the tragic remains of the young war-widow was not amongst them.

He'd parked his car by the lych-gate and was making his way down towards it when something reminiscent of that *turn-again-Anderson* feeling, which he'd had previously when passing in the car, was now urging him to turn-again to face a corner of the graveyard, which he'd knowingly overlooked.

Guy had given that bit of hallowed territory a miss because there seemed to be an absence of tombstones and the whole, neglected area was dense and overgrown with thorns. Now, as he unwittingly moved in that direction, the wild framework of brambles seemed predestined to receive him. He began to push his way into the depths of thorny undergrowth towards the low corner walls of the churchyard. Soon, he was up to his waste in thistles and a vigorous array of blackthorn, hawthorn and some thousand-and-one other thorns. He waded, undaunted, like a maniac as the barbs jabbed through his clothes into his skin, pulling and snagging at his sweater until he was totally ensnared within the tangled mess. He cursed as the thorns bit into his flesh, bringing tiny spurts of blood to the surface of his skin – but then his foot hit the immovable hardness of granite – and in that moment, he almost knew his search was over.

His groping hands bled as he fought the encasement of briars guarding the hidden tomb.

The sudden depth of cold, damp, rotting leaves soothed away the pain as he delved deeper and deeper to finally touch the white stonework. His fingers trembled as they caressed the curve of the jutting headstone, which was getting its first glimpse of daylight through decades of rambling and rotting thorns. Guy knelt amongst them to read the neat, black engraving of the simple epitaph.

To the memory of
MARY ANN BARKER
Of
APRIL COTTAGE
Aged 25 years
Who departed this life
On
April 6th 1943
Rest in Peace.

25

When Guy Anderson, the star, stepped out on stage later that evening to give old Henry that salutary slap-on-the-back, a rapturous applause from the first night audience was only silenced by his opening line: "Ezra Jackson, I haven't seen you in years!"

In the guise of the suave Trevor Adams, he now relinquished all thoughts of Mary Ann Barker as he strode the boards in the stylish manner of the professional that he was. Indeed, after the frustrations of delving into the past for the majority of the day, it was almost a relief to sink into the comfortable brogues of Adams, a freelance writer with a cause, whose self-opinionated views land him into all kinds of trouble, including murder, but who - in the end, inevitably conquers all; not least the irrepressible Vanda Fairchild who falls into his arms like a rag doll.

Delia Davidson's Vanda was given more than her usual amount of flair and fervour that night as she seductively held onto him in the clinches, and remorselessly pressed herself against him at the down-centre position. Dee enjoyed her advantage over the audience and made the most of demonstrating to all those adoring females out there, the absolute claim she had on that man; the object of their futile desires. She alluringly played out her part with the utmost professionalism, but always with the hidden intentions of reaching him in reality – a goal she was fairly hopeful of, but she realised it was going to take time. Guy had undergone a great deal of stress and, in his own words, needed time and space. If she rushed things, she would lose him, so she contented herself with bringing Vanda closer to Trevor.

    His arms were round her now as they neared the end of the performance and, amidst the merging of melting greasepaint, she responded unwaveringly to the demands of the script, which had conveniently underlined the need for a lengthy and intimate kiss – and so, she had allowed him to extract every ounce of her vitality until the final curtain, like sudden death, dropped on her limp orgasmic state. It was all over again and like a puppet, she was being heedlessly thrust into the line-up of fellow actors who, with gripping hands held aloft, were sweeping themselves into the first of several bows.

26

"Guy, love! What on earth have you been doing to your hands?" Oberon asked, wafting away Henry's cigar smoke. "Where did you get those scratches?"

"Fighting off the females, I'd say, 'Bron!" Henry interjected, chuckling into his beer.

They were relaxing in the green-room, which was bleak and basic. But it was sanctity from the autograph-hunters, who were still milling around the stage-door, hoping to catch Guy Anderson as he left. By contrast, the lesser known members of the cast had blithely rushed off to mingle with the patrons up in the balcony-bar before it closed. Dee had been creaming-off her greasepaint in the dressing room and was hurriedly making her way to the green-room.

"I'm almost certain that the audience noticed. They *must* have noticed..." Oberon chided. "You look as though you've been fighting off a tiger, dear!"

"Exactly what I thought!" Dee said, making an even more ravishing entrance than she'd done on stage. "And just who has been getting their claws into you this time?"

"Just a bit of a thorny subject, which doesn't concern any of you!" Guy said, hoping that would be the end of it.

"Let me see!" Dee demanded, dropping into the seat beside him and taking his hand in hers, raising his sleeves. "Good God, Guy, what have you been up to?"

"Nothing!" he said, resentfully.

"Nothing!?" she admonished. "These scratches need medical attention!"

"Rubbish, woman!" he gnarled, snatching his hands from her grasp. "If you must know, I got myself entangled in a pile of thorns in a churchyard. When I was a kid, I was always covered in scratches like this and nothing's changed, okay!?"

"And what were you doing in a churchyard?"

"Walking."

"Walking in a churchyard? Nobody does that, Guy!" Dee said, flatly.

"Certainly not through piles of thorns, they don't!" Oberon concurred, tossing back his quiff of blonde hair.

"They don't, but I do!" Guy persisted.

"You expect us to believe that?" Dee went on.

"You can believe anything you like, my darling. Now then, can we leave it there, please?"

The two of them exchanged muted glances whilst Henry wisely changed the subject. "Went jolly well tonight, don't you think? Damn good audience, I thought! Bloody good!"

"I was assured by the local press that we'd get a good write up" Oberon said, flicking casually through the worn pages of a fashion magazine. "And they tell me that the *Evening Sentinel* has a pretty good circulation! Apparently, it goes all over North Staffordshire and South Cheshire. When the photographer left, he told me that the lady theatre-critic was completely besotted with the play!"

"Besotted with *him*, more like it!" Henry nodded with a good-natured smirk in Guy's direction, discarding his cigar stump into his empty beer glass before rising to his feet. "Well, I don't know about the rest of you, but I'm ready to make a move. Thankful to say I don't have to worry about facing fans at the stage-door anymore. Cheers, everyone!"

"Bye, Henry" Guy said, staring absently at the raspberry red walls of the green-room. He was contemplating retiring back to April Cottage himself, but decided to give it a few more minutes. He wasn't prepared to admit it to a soul, but the thought of returning to the cottage was far more disconcerting than the thought of going out to face the fans.

"Well…" Oberon exclaimed, checking his watch and replacing the magazine onto the pile. "I'll go and see if Ronnie has finished fiddling with the tabs; it's time we were all leaving. Shall I get someone to bring your car round to the side-exit, Guy?"

"Thanks, 'Bron. I'd be grateful for that."

"Don't worry about me, Oberon. I'll just plough through the mob" Dee called sulkily after the production manager as he left the room. If she was trying to make a point, Guy wasn't aware of it. He was thinking about the very real prospect of having to face the ghostly and, hitherto, unseen presence of Mary Ann Barker.

27

Why, in God's name, am I even contemplating going back?

"What's the matter with you, Guy?" Dee asked with concern, noticing a certain unease about his person.

"Nothing, Dee. Just tired, I suppose."

She leaned closer to him, touching his face with one hand and sensitively tracing the lines of torn skin on the back of his hand with the other.

"Come back to the hotel and I'll dress those wounds for you. We could have some coffee and sandwiches sent up?"

In view of the alternative, Guy was tempted, but found himself too weary to make a decision. Eventually, he found some words. "We could go out for a meal one night, Dee, but I'd better be getting back to the cottage tonight, it's late."

She dropped his hand like a hot cake and stood over him. "Do you know, Guy Anderson, I get the very distinct impression that you are being rather pig-headed about this precious cottage of yours! I get the feeling that you are simply putting up with it just to be obstinate! Why don't you admit it? It's a dump isn't it! And you wish you hadn't taken it, don't you?"

"You couldn't be more wrong!"

"Then why are you being so evasive about it?"

"I'm not! Try to understand, Dee – I just want to get away from everything and everybody – so I take a country retreat for a week. What's so hard to understand about wanting seclusion?"

"What's right with it? If you want to live like a bloody monk, you should retreat to a monastery, not a country-cottage!"

Making no comment, he rose to take his jacket from the back of a chair. She watched his scarred fingers fumbling to fasten the single button, and with all agitation gone, she was there to fasten it for him. Next, her palms were brushing down over the smooth lapels and her painted-nail fingers idly picking imaginary bits from the padded shoulders as she gazed up wistfully into the coolness of his eyes. "Let me go with you, Guy – to the cottage. Please, Guy!" She ran her forefinger along the curve of his moustache and it quivered as it lingered on the edge of his mouth before pushing its way inside. His teeth closed over it, holding it there in a controlled, gentle bite, which had her whole body responding with all the eroticism she dared to allow.

Guy felt himself weakening as his arms closed around her; he'd always known that she was his for the taking. Should her take her now? She *was* a beautiful woman. In view of his mounting reluctance to return to the cottage alone, it was a real temptation. If he was to take someone back with him, maybe the awesome presence within those walls would drift away, or at least seem less obvious. Delia's hot breath was provocatively invading his ear, and her fingers were stealthily straying beneath the lining of his jacket.

28

At that awesome moment, Oberon made his entrance with all the timing and stage-presence of a bad fairy! "Sorry to intrude, Guy love, but they've brought your car round to the side entrance. If you come now, we can get you away from the fans!"

Delia's expression dropped to the floorboards as Guy now held her at an arms-length. "Look, darling, leave it there for now. I'd better go. I'll see you tomorrow night and we'll make arrangements then, okay?"

In view of Oberon's insensitive presence, she could hardly protest as Guy kissed her quickly on the cheek before hurrying out. Oberon was about to follow him but was recalled by a feline hiss.

"Did you want to say something, Dee?" he asked, popping his head around the door.

"Yes! Thanks for being a shit!"

"You're welcome!" he said with a wry smirk before closing the door. Oberon was more than familiar with Dee's all-too-obvious feelings towards Guy. He breathed in with contentment, before following Guy to his car.

29

It was a jittery moment for Guy when the cold weightiness of that enormous key turned in the April Cottage door-lock. With much trepidation, he entered the interior darkness, but the brilliant wattage of a light bulb, plus the glow of a hastily lit fire, soon eased the foreboding situation. Minutes later, he was slowly unwinding with a glass of Beaujolais as he watched the rolling credits of some outdated film. He was only able to get the one channel and the late weather forecast finally drove him to the switch.

A contrasting silence followed as he stared into the comforting flicker of firelight. *'She wails each night before midnight'*. The words had been careering through his psyche ever since he'd heard them. Normally, Guy would have shrugged off such nonsense with contempt, but on the basis of what he had since learned, he had to admit to himself that there was some cause for credence.

What in God's name am I doing here if this place is haunted? Why do I feel so motivated to return? There were hundreds of places to choose from and he could afford any of them! Why was he in this God-forsaken little hovel? He remained there in his seat, staring into the stillness of the room and listening to the unaccountable sounds of silence.

Since the day he'd first arrived at April Cottage, he'd felt a very real empathy within the atmosphere; an unexplainable belonging. Whatever it was he was hearing as he sat there with the glow of firelight on his face - whatever it was he was feeling; he knew instinctively that he wasn't alone.

30

Before ascending the narrow stairway, Guy paused silently by the closed sitting-room door. There was a stifling, almost clammy silence, and for a brief moment he felt a slight compulsion to open the door, but as he touched the wooden knob, he decided against it and climbed the wooden hills instead. The carpeted treads creaked softly beneath his feet and as he neared the top, the totally unexpected ringing of the telephone pierced the silence, causing him to trip into an undignified sprawl over the topmost step.

Picking himself up and rubbing his shins, he limped his way back down the stairs threatening to crucify the caller. He burst angrily into the sitting-room and stumbled over the hearth-rug in an effort to reach the phone. Guy reached out for the receiver, but paused for a moment as he suddenly realised that a phone call at such a late hour was indeed a strange occurrence – and with all the freakish events of late, he wondered what the latest capricious contingency might be. *Perhaps ghostly cries or screams of anguish down the phone?*

Maybe something more supernatural, beyond comprehension? Maybe just silence? His temporary fears were laid to rest as he lifted the receiver to the unmistakable voice of Delia.

"Guy?"

"Yes! Of course it's me! Who d'you think it is – pissing Frankenstein?" What the hell do you want at this time of night?"

"I want you, Guy. I really do want you, darling!" Dee said, bluntly.

"Well if you want me in one piece, you could choose a better time to ring – I almost broke my neck on the stairs just now! No, I'm not in bed – I'm just going and it's time you were too!"

"I *am* in bed, Guy. I can't sleep" she whined almost pathetically.

"Well, take a tablet! Take two!"

"I don't want tablets! I want you!"

"Listen, Dee…"

"I want you now!"

"Don't be silly, Dee! I'm going to bed!"

"Come back to the hotel, Guy. Please!"

"You must be joking!? Or is this some kind of revenge?"

"I'm not joking! If you don't come to me now, I'm going to die!"

"You're not going to die! You're going to sleep – and hopefully, so am I!" He flopped down despairingly into the depths of the old armchair. "I told you that we'd fix something up for tomorrow night."

"Tomorrow will be too late..." her voice trailed off.

"Oh, stop being so dramatic, woman! Leave Vanda Fairchild at the theatre where she belongs. You're no more like her than I am like that dreadful Adams fellow!" Now Dee was crying on the other end of the phone. Guy's anger softened. "I'm sorry, Dee. I didn't mean to upset you. That's the last thing I want. It's just that you're there and I'm here, so let's be sensible about it, shall we?"

"I don't want to be sensible. I want to be with you!"

"It's far too late, my darling!" It was like speaking to a child.

"It's not too late; it's only just gone midnight! You could be here in twenty minutes, there's no traffic about at this time of night."

"Out of the question, Dee! I'm over the limit; I've had several glasses of wine – you know my weakness for Beaujolais!"

"And *you* know *my* weakness for you!"

"I honestly don't know what you see in me, Delia. I'm past all that kind of thing."

"You'll never be past it, Guy Anderson. Let me prove it to you? Come to the hotel, right now. Please, Guy, say you'll come…"

Guy didn't *say* anything. He didn't say anything because a sudden heady whiff of perfume had drifted into the room again, infusing the atmosphere with such allurement that he was almost in a trance-like state.

"I feel so deprived without you here, Guy. I'm lying here in this enormous bed, practically naked. The sheets feel so cold that I'm shuddering. I need you here to hold me. Guy? Are you still there?"

"Yes" he murmured, abstractedly drawn to whatever situation was now unfolding by the window.

"I know you feel something for me. I knew tonight, when we were in the green-room with your arms around me. I want to feel them around me now, Guy. I'm so desperate for you that I keep touching myself – you know what I mean, don't you? I'm touching myself right now, and I want you to feel what I'm feeling. Tell me that it's your hands that I can feel moving over my body; your hands closing over my breasts. Tell me! …TELL ME!" She breathed down the phone with an urgency that would have driven most men wild.

Guy was oblivious of what she was saying. He was utterly transfixed by the sudden movement of the curtain, which was now being mysteriously elevated, until the darkened glass behind it was starkly revealed. Every nerve in his body was rigid with fear. He was completely incapable of movement. He could only stare at the swift aura of light at the window, gradually developing and shaping itself into existence; the slender figure and form of a young woman looking upwards and out. A delicate hand holding back the curtain awaiting someone's return. The decorated clips shimmered where the golden blonde hair was taken up at the sides; the rest of it gently falling onto the back of the elegantly padded-shoulders of the frock, which skimmed down to closely drape the slim ankles.

"We're so right for each other, Guy! Do you believe in fate? I do!" Dee's voice droned on distantly, far beyond the bounds of Guy's ear. "Getting the part of Vanda was a miracle come true for me, Guy. That was fate. I really can't help the way I feel about you. Please say something... Guy? Are you still there, Guy?"

"Dee?" Guy was suddenly aware of his temporary daze. "Dee! Darling?"

"Yes, Guy?" she asked, excited by the distinct tremor in his voice.

"There's someone by the window!" His voice had dropped three tones lower.

"What!? What do you mean, *someone* by the window?"

"She's standing by the window! She's here in the room with me!" His words were almost incoherent.

"Who's *she?*" She demanded with a raised voice. "Who the hell is *she?*"

"You won't believe me if I tell you."

"Are you trying to say that you've got another woman there with you?"

"No, of course not!" he answered strangely, unable to divert his eyes from the graceful transparency at the window. "No, not a woman. Just a girl."

"Just a girl!?" Now, there was venom in her voice.

"She's going, Dee. She's going!" He said it again, more slowly, as he witnessed the figure mystically dispersing into the atmosphere, leaving nothing but the waft of the curtain as it fell back into place below the sill.

"Oh, well, that's alright then if she's going, isn't it? Have you paid her for services rendered?" Hell was now having its fury.

Guy couldn't speak and the was a long ominous pause, which only provoked her more. "Well, whoever she is, she's obviously preferable to me! Probably one of those inane little fans of yours!"

Guy was still incapable of responding; all his senses were drawn to the spot where the girl had stood and where he felt she remained, unseen. Dee was still going on at the other end of the line but he didn't seem to be aware of it. All he could hear was gentle, soft weeping - though not much more than a sigh, to him, it was so touchingly poignant that it seemed to penetrate the innermost depths of his being.

"Please, don't cry!" he said with the utmost contrition.

"I'm not bloody crying, you bastard!" Delia sent the vibrations of her anger into his ear drum. "How on earth could you let me go on talking to you the way I did when you were having it off with some cheap little shit of a girl! You absolute bastard! I'll never forgive you! Never!" Her voice broke into a crescendo of violent sobbing as she slammed the phone down.

31

Early next morning, after a dreadful night's sleep, Guy had been called to the Five Towns Hotel for an emergency meeting with Oberon, who was flapping about the place like an old hen.

"Whatever is going on between you two is nothing to do with me – I know that, Guy love, but if you don't do something, we're in trouble! We've all done our best to calm her down but it's hopeless, dear. She won't listen to me or Ronnie, and the rest of the cast won't have any more to do with it – and I don't blame them! She simply wipes the floor with anyone who tries to reason with her. She's absolutely inconsolable!" He indignantly flipped a bit of fluff from his scarlet shirt. "I wouldn't have dreamed of dragging you out here this morning if there had been the merest possibility of calming her down, and coaxing her into changing her mind about walking-out on the play. I've seen some theatrical tantrums in my time, dear, but I can assure you this one takes some beating. When I endeavoured to broach the subject over breakfast, all I got was a spate of obscenities and a load of abuse. When I put it to her that all of this was going to result in further bad publicity for you, she picked up my plate of organic muesli and threw it at that bust of Josiah Wedgwood! That one, which stands on a pillar in the corner of the room! I was mortified with embarrassment, Guy love, can you imagine?"

"Stupid cow!" Guy stifled the words under his breath with a sip of black coffee. By courtesy of the management, the two of them were privately ensconced into a corner of the Potter's lounge. A distraught Oberon had arranged for a tray of coffee and toast to be sent in, and had requested for a Do-Not-Disturb sign to be hung on the door for at least thirty minutes.

"So, we're all hoping that you will be able to save the day by popping up to her suite. If *you* can't get through to her, nobody can! She's threatening to leave today and I suspect that she will be stalling just long enough for you to make an appearance. I don't have to tell you, dear boy, that if she does leave, we're in the most horrendous mess!" He poured himself another cup of coffee before going on. "Angie Townsend was the best understudy we had and we're not going to get her back after the way she was insulted at the Hippodrome. So, I certainly think you'll need the kid-glove charm, dear, or there'll be no show!"

Guy sipped the rest of his coffee and replaced the cup in its saucer. "I don't know how I'm going to be able to deal with her, 'Bron. How do I start?"

"Don't ask me...you're far better equipped to deal with that than me."

"You want to place a wager on that?"

"Well, everyone knows she wants to get you into the conjugal bed, love!"

"Not a chance!" Guy rose and wandered over to the window to look out over the dismal view of work-a-day traffic moving slowly along in the rain.

Oberon watched and patiently waited for the leading-man to make the next move. He'd seen more than enough of the leading-lady for one day. After violating the breakfast-bar with her wrath, and following it with a furious fracas in the foyer before making a tearful departure to her room, it didn't take a genius to figure out what had been going on – or not going on, as was the case. And now, Guy's nonplus attitude to it all seemed to be confirming his worst fears; there must have been an almighty bust-up!

"I've seen all this coming, Guy love, we all have! When you'd left for the cottage on Saturday, she did nothing but mope around the hotel all day, being utterly cantankerous and most unreasonable with all and sundry. Old Henry, bless his heart, took her out to an expensive Chinese restaurant, and according to him, she talked about you for the entire evening; she even had the audacity to tell him that she wished you were there in his place – how's that for ungracious behaviour, dear?"

Guy's disgruntled reply was indistinguishable against the tapestry-draped window as he continued to listen to the production manager's camp voice twittering on.

"When they got back here, Henry went off to the bar, and then she came tripping up to my room; she didn't give a hoot that Ronnie and I were having one of our private conversations. She simply stood in the doorway, demanding that I should give her directions to your cottage. She was coming over to see you, at that time of night! I knew how you'd feel about that, so I tried to put her off by telling her that the cottage was cold and damp. It was then that she insisted on having your telephone number."

"And can you blame me? She rang me then and she rang me last night. Both calls were after midnight!"

"What did she want?"

"What do *you* think!?"

"You poor love! What a travesty!" Oberon said, tossing back the quiff of hair. "Well, it seems to me, dear, that it's only going to take a few words of remission from you – and you could save the day for all of us! Just fob her off with a few words about being out-of-sorts last night, and promise her something better for tonight – and Hey Presto, Guy love, she'll be eating out of the palm of your hand!"

"It's not quite that easy, 'Bron. Dee is quite convinced that I had another woman with me last night."

"What nonsense!"

"Not exactly, 'Bron. Not exactly."

32

"Not exactly? What do you mean, *not exactly?*" Oberon demanded.

"I mean, there *was* someone there, but…"

"Please, Guy love, please put me out of my misery, dear, don't tell me Roxanne's trying to make a comeback?"

"Spare me that! She'd be the last person I'd want to see!"

"The saints be praised for that! So, who was it? Come on, dear. You know I'm the soul of discretion where you are concerned. Anything you tell me, it's confidential. It has to be!" Despite Oberon's passion for a good gossip, Guy knew he could place his trust in his *Fairy Godmother*.

"It was Mary Ann Barker." Guy returned to his seat, lifted the *cafetiere* and poured himself another cup of coffee.

"Who?"

"Mary Ann Barker…"

"Do I know her? The name doesn't ring a bell. Is she in the theatre?"

"No!" Guy snapped out the word.

APRIL COTTAGE

Oberon was getting the kind of signals that made him feel distinctly uncomfortable. Guy's blank look spelt all kinds of trouble. Just what had he been up to? Surely not womanising again!?

"You're not getting yourself involved again, are you, Guy love?"

"No way!"

"If you are, I tremble to think what the tabloids would make of it! They can't wait for a sequel! Please don't give them one!"

"I could give them a sequel alright, but they'd never believe me and neither would you!"

"Try me!"

"Very well. She's a ghost."

"Who is?"

"Mary Ann Barker is!"

"You're right, dear, they wouldn't believe it, and neither do I! You'll have to do better than that!"

"How's this then?" Guy looked up over the rim of his coffee cup, his sleek dark eyebrows scanning a candid expression. "Yesterday, I was standing knee-deep in thorns at a woman's graveside – a woman who had died in the forties. Last night I spoke to Dee on the phone, and that same woman was standing in the room!"

Oberon was now extremely concerned for the production's leading man; the poor dear was losing it! Recent publicity must surely have taken its toll.

"She was standing by the window, looking out. I saw her before in the bedroom but I thought I was dreaming. Now I know for certain that it was no dream! I could see her as clearly as I'm seeing you now!"

"My dear, sweet boy, are you telling me that prima-donna Davidson is walking-out on us on the premise that you think you've seen a ghost? My God! Is there anyone in theatre that hasn't seen a ghost? We thrive on the assumption that we have!"

"Yes, I see what you're saying, 'Bron, but unfortunately, Dee thinks my ghost is a flesh and blood prostitute!"

Oberon, not taking any of this seriously, looked at his watch and leaned across the table towards Guy. "Well if that's the case, and if you wish to keep your leading-lady, you're going to have to make her see otherwise. And soon, dear!" They rose from their seats simultaneously and made for the exit.

"Leave it to me then, 'Bron."

"And if I were you, Guy love, I'd be thinking very seriously of getting out of that cottage!"

"And if you were me, 'Bron, you'd be going up to Dee's room instead of me! Any advice in that direction, 'Bron?"

"I wouldn't know where to start" he replied quietly. "Good luck, Guy love!"

He stood anxiously watching from the carpeted foyer as Guy took the first flight of marble-clad steps in preference to the lift.

33

He stopped just below the first-floor landing where tall stained-glass windows scaled the face of the embossed walls to the upper loftiness beyond. Despite that encompassment of Victorian grandeur, he was still unable to dispel from his mind that vision of Mary Ann Barker and the sound of her sorrowful weeping. He continued his climb to the second floor.

Dee's room was tenth along the corridor. He glanced for a moment at the Do-Not-Disturb sign, before his knuckles bumped against the thick panelled door. There was no response. He hadn't expected there to be. He knocked again with more force – still no response. Casually taking a pen from his pocket he detached the hanging sign from the brass door knob and beneath the 'Do-Not-Disturb', he wrote in his stylish handwriting *'unless it happens to be Guy Anderson'*.

He pushed the card under the door and waited – and waited. A solitary figure on the long corridor of closed doors, Guy stood with a blank expression, suspecting that she was standing on the other side of the door, waiting for him to knock again – and probably taking some pleasure in his unease of the situation. He then surmised that if he didn't knock again she would be wondering if he'd given up and gone – then perhaps her curiosity would get the better of her and she might then open the door just to check that he had gone. *Worth a try.* He remained quietly outside the closed door. After a lengthy wait, he was rewarded by the sounds of the door being unlocked. She eventually opened the door to find his tall frame confronting her. She tried to close the door but he firmly propelled her back into the room. The door swung itself to a close behind him.

"Get out, you bastard!" She fought at him with her fists until her wrists were in his grip and she was being forced into the centre of the large room.

"Delia…"

"Don't you 'Delia' me, get out!"

"Dee! Calm down and listen to me!"

"I won't listen to you ever again, Guy Anderson! Never again!"

Facing her hostility, he increased his grip on her wrists. "Leave the dramatics behind, you little fool, and for once in your life just listen!"

"I'm leaving you and the play, d'you hear? I'm leaving!"

"You're staying right here and listening to me!"

There was another bout of struggling before she was forced into submission by his gentle strength and overall patience. He held her firmly at arms-length, piercing her eyes with his and finally dabbing the tears from her cheeks with his fingers.

"You do realise that all of this is over nothing, don't you? Absolutely nothing! You've been letting your imagination run away with you again, haven't you? You didn't give me any chance last night to explain things to you. You simply slammed the phone down and when I rang you back, it was off the hook!"

"What did you expect me to do? You said you had some woman with you – a girl, you said! Who was she then, this little *Miss Innocent*?"

"I'll tell you if you try not to intervene and get yourself into a state. That's why I'm here, damn it! I'm here to try and make you realise how stupid all of this is!" He walked her over to a chair and she sat down, looking up at him with a child-like expression.

"Go on then, put me out of my misery!" Dee sulked.

"You remember when I said someone was by the window? Well whilst you were talking to me on the phone - this person was at the window, looking in. It shocked me at that time of night."

"But you said she was *in* the room, not outside!"

"I could see she was obviously distressed and I gestured to her to come in at the front door. You were still on the phone and she could see that, so she waited. I was trying to let you know that she was there because of our private conversation. I was about to tell you that I'd ring you back once I'd sorted out whatever her problem was, but then of course, you jumped to all kinds of conclusions and I couldn't get a word in before you slammed the phone down on me! When I eventually rang you back, the phone was off the hook!"

"I see...and what happened after I'd put the phone down?"

Guy walked away to avoid her questioning eyes. He was used to learning lines, not constructing them. Now it was a case of lying through his teeth to save the day – and so he continued to make it up as he went along. "It seemed she'd nearly gone off the road with a puncture. It's very lonely round there and she'd seen that the cottage lights were on and assumed she could ring for help. She was very frightened and quite a few miles from her home. She said she'd been to some religious convention with her friends. I told her she could ring her parents but she said her mother was invalid and her father had died. I finished up walking her back to the car, mending her puncture and sending her on her way. That is once I'd managed to push her car off the grass verge."

"Didn't she recognise you?"

"I don't think anyone would have recognised me last night. I was in a bit of a state. Luckily, she wasn't the sort to recognise me anyway; quite a timid little thing she was. I felt sorry for her."

"Nonsense! She had the handsome Guy Anderson as her knight in shining armour. Whatever time did you get to bed, you poor darling?"

"Didn't take me very long. Soon after one, at a guess."

"I'm so sorry, Guy" she said, rising and moving towards him. "I've made an utter fool of myself, haven't I?" She walked over to the bed when an open suitcase lay with her clothes strewn around it. He watched as she closed the case and placed it on the nearby stand. Next, she returned her dresses and skirts to the wardrobe whilst Guy felt a sudden relief that his mission to tame-the-beast had clearly been successful. "I think I'll have to take myself in hand, don't you? I didn't sleep a wink last night, I must look frightful!"

He began to hand her the clothes and shoes as she put them away. He couldn't help noticing the darkness beneath her eyes, knowing that it was because of tears and lack of sleep. The round glass ashtray on her bedside table was littered with half-smoked cigarettes. She saw him looking and quickly tipped the dog-ends into the waste basket.

"Dee, how about me taking you out for a late meal tonight after the performance?"

"You think a meal will solve everything, don't you, Guy?" she mused, sarcastically.

"No, it's just one way of saying I'm sorry…"

"Well, there are better ways!" she said seductively as she sauntered slowly towards him. "You *could* kiss me…"

34

His mouth closed deliciously over hers – and the thrilling pressure of his body against her was all she needed. Now that she had him in the privacy of her room, there would never be a better chance.

She caught the sight of their reflections in the mirror-fronted wardrobe and bewitchingly turned his attention towards it; urging him to gaze at their images as she seductively moved in-front of him. He watched, allowing her to draw her hands down over her shoulders, enticing his fingers to stray beneath the jacket of her neat little navy suit. Her fingers lowered to loosen the jacket buttons as her green eyes met with his within the framed reflection. Her jacket fell open and the creaminess of her midriff was highlighted by the fitted waistband of the deep-blue skirt and the even deeper-blue of her lacy bra. She could see that his eyes were now riveted on the fullness beneath the bra – and excited by the power she was beginning to have over him, her fingers moved deftly beneath the jacket to remove it. She watched rapturously as his hands closed over her nakedness.

Guy was only too aware that he was being manipulated; it was a dangerous game to play, but he was ready to play it as he watched the pencil skirt fall to the floor. Stepping out of it, she turned to face him as her hands with painted nails eased down the brief bits of lace from hips to ankles, daintily kicking them aside. Wearing nothing now but the jacket top, she stood away from him, provocatively inviting his gaze. The pale silkiness of her body was so refreshingly different to the burnt-orange of Roxanne. It was the English rose versus the tiger-lily. She was a few years older than his ex-wife and he found the slight maturity pleasing.

Roxanne had always demanded too much; always a lengthy foreplay whereby he was expected to display and sustain a masculine hunger of monumental proportions. In the beginning, of course, it had been sheer mutual enjoyment. What man wouldn't enjoy having to satisfy the endless cravings of a dusky beauty with all that torrid passion thrown in? Eventually, however, the decline in his output had sent her into the muscular embrace of a stallion-dancer, many years his junior.

Dee removed the short jacket and walked over towards the bed. She was aware that her every step was gaining his admiration. It took a woman like Dee to retain that sheer, classic, womanly elegance when completely starkers!

"To think..." she said provokingly, "to think that only minutes ago I was preparing to walk-out on you, and now I'm inviting you to share my bed!"

He moved towards her and lowered his eyes over the contours of her body. "You couldn't walk out on me – what would Trevor Adams do without you?"

"I don't give a hoot about Trevor Adams" she drawled, rubbing the palms of her hands against the reveres of his tweed jacket. "It's the *real* man I want. It's you!"

35

His fingers were stranding through the natural waves in her hair to the nape of neck, and then down to the sloping line of her bare shoulders; his hands slowly but firmly pressurizing her to sit on the edge of the bed. He stood over her and began to remove his jacket.

"Let me do it!" Dee demanded. Her hands reached up inside his jacket and her fingers were undoing the shirt buttons, one by one, until the knotted tie hung down over a mere sprinkling of dark hairs on his chest. She pressed her face into the spicy warmth of his body and could feel the leather belt on his jeans digging into her breasts. Holding onto him, she pulled herself to her feet, burying her nakedness into the roughness of the loosed jacket.

"This isn't Vanda and Trevor, darling..." she uttered, undoing the buckle and wantonly removing the belt from his jeans. "This is Dee and Guy!" The belt was tossed into the air. "Would you care for a preview performance, sir?"

It was some performance. She engulfed every part of him with her hands and mouth, removing the clothes from his body as she went, pulling him onto the bed where they lay side by side, sharing a prime moment of genuine desire. Frantically she urged him onto his back, bringing the gentle weight of her slender hips down over his, and engaging her intimate warmth where he needed it most.

36

"I can't help the way I feel about you, Guy Anderson" she whispered feverishly into his ear with a succession of uncontrollable movements. "I love you. I love you so much. Say you want me!"

He said it almost aggressively and meant it. She was pressing down on him with such an urgency that they were soon raging out of control towards the kind of rapturous insanity that is hellbent on reaching a climax – but for Guy, the climax came too soon.

"Sorry, Dee. Oh hell, I'm sorry!

"Sorry why?" she said, smothering his face with kisses.

Sorry. All the lost emotions were in that one word, and he felt the burning tears oozing into the corners of his eyes.

"But it was wonderful!" she breathed. For once, she was aware of a magnificent feeling of power over him as she felt the physical deflation being withdrawn from within. "Much too wonderful to last!"

Guy had fought against his inadequacy and lost. He felt impotent and foolish, but Dee was holding onto him with sustained ardour.

"Having you like this is…is…is everything to me!" she said, consolingly. "Having you here in my bed is divine intervention as far as I'm concerned. I love you, Guy. No-one could love you more!"

"God knows why!" he muttered and reaching for his shirt. Roxanne was right, wasn't she? I *am* a complete waste of space in the bedroom!"

Dee shot off the bed towards him. "Forget her! She didn't deserve you!" Her fingers were buttoning up his shirt as she spoke. "Next time will be so much more wonderful, I promise!". She looked up into his face with the most loving expression. "Next time will be at night, and I shall go on making love to you until you fall asleep in my arms!"

37

As Guy walked out of the lift, Oberon was waiting by the foyer bar with Ronnie. The two of them turned anxiously to face him.

"How's it gone?" Oberon couldn't wait to know.

"No problem!"

"You mean, she's okay now"

"Yep – fine!"

"You've been ages, Guy love. Ronnie and I were getting quite concerned, weren't we, Ronnie? You must have had to spin her quite a yarn?"

"Not really. Don't worry 'Bron. I don't think you'll be having any more problems with our lovely leading-lady – so I'll get back to my country retreat for a few hours before tonight's performance."

"It's thanks to you, Guy love, that there's going to *be* a performance! Judging by the turbulent mood she was in this morning I thought we'd lost everything! Didn't *you,* Ronnie? Heaven only knows how you managed to calm her down, dear, but I can assure you – it didn't come a moment too soon!"

That's where you're wrong! Guy thought. With a wry smile, he gave Oberon an avuncular wink as he whisked his way out through the revolving doors.

38

Guy decided to take the remains of his lunch down to George's cats. He'd opened a can of salmon and made a pile of sandwiches but only managed to eat one of them. He'd put it down to the box of chocolates he'd greedily demolished as he'd driven back from the hotel - sex for elevenses had boosted his appetite if not his ego.

Walking down the lane that afternoon was indescribably uplifting. It was really the first warm day of spring and by contrast to the way he was feeling, everything seemed so young and alive. He tried his utmost to push the rest of the world away as his footsteps took him along the rustic track towards Holly Cottage, but even through that hidden heaven of thrusting hedgerows with its blossomed foliage and tumultuous hordes of birds and bees, his mind was still pondering the inevitable; just how much would Dee be demanding of him now? Her testament of love had been declared and, God help him, he had to admit he'd found her devastatingly irresistible. He could see the web being woven and found some crumb of comfort in what she'd said as he'd left her room:

"I know how tentative you must feel about starting a new relationship. I think we're both equally aware of the pitfalls, aren't we?" and then she'd kissed him again before jauntily buttoning up her neat little jacket, adding "so let's take it from here and see what evolves. Promising idea?" An endearing, childlike expression had then searched his handsome features for the right response.

"Good idea!" he'd replied.

"That's alright then!" she'd breathed ecstatically.

He'd gained some relief from knowing there was still a husband somewhere in the background; she still wore his ring – and there was a grown-up son who occasionally kept in touch; occasionally being the operative word. Dee, however, never spoke to him about either of them and it was obvious that whatever they'd been to her in the past, they were of little importance to her now.

He paused beneath an old oak, where rambling ivy had relentlessly climbed and twisted itself around the sturdy trunk with such intensity that there was more ivy leaf than bark. Guy stared upwards into the heart of the tree's greenery with the thought of that mighty oak standing rooted to the spot and being utterly incapable of preventing the intruding tendrils crushing the heart and soul out of it. *There's a lesson in there somewhere*, Guy thought.

As he moved on into the shadows of the lane, the ephemeral vision of Mary Ann Barker returned again. The graphic portrayal of the young woman at the window, the smell of her perfume and the sound of her weeping, which had so haunted his senses through the waking and sleeping hours of the night were now possessing him once again - in the broad light of day!

With apprehension, he contemplated the arrival of the coming night. The idea of abandoning the cottage and going to stay with the rest of the cast at the hotel seemed to be infinitely sensible. It was inevitable that the entire company would be pressurizing him to do so, none more so than Dee. Guy winced at the thought of coping with too many twice-nightly performances with the leading-lady. If this morning's little preview was anything to go by, he doubted if he could stay the course. At least Mary Ann Barker wouldn't be making any similar demands on him; ghosts may scare the hell out of you but they can't touch you. *Can they?* Perhaps if he kept off the Beaujolais, the illusion might not be so alarming. *Was it an illusion?* Guy knew enough about himself to know that it wasn't - then again, he thought he'd known enough about himself to believe that he would never see a ghost. Always the sceptic with his fellow actors, with their ridiculous tales of gruesome spectres destined to wander the walls and upper galleries of the many old theatres they'd visited. Macbeth and Hamlet and the odd monk were some of the more favoured ones – and only yesterday, he'd heard one of them talking about their present venue, the Theatre Royal, having a ghost; that of a night-watchman who had supposedly perished in the fire, which had once gutted an earlier building on the same site. Amusedly, he toyed with improbability of it all until the track took him round the sharp bend and there, looking far less formidable by the day, the mysterious pebble-dashed cottage, which curiosity had brought him to see again. The cats, who were only an excuse, would surely have understood his motives.

39

It was undoubtedly a replica of something he'd seen before, but *where and when?* Dismissing the query from his mind, he ventured towards the small house, which, though dingy with neglect, was oddly appealing in the afternoon sunshine. He passed the spot where the cat had previously given him such a hostile reception in the gloom of that Sunday evening, scanning warily yet briefly under those same bushes and finding nothing but rotting leaves.

The small wicket-gate was hinged to its post with thick pieces of frayed string, which caused it to hang at an odd angle. A muffled clanking noise was coming from the rear of the cottage and he assumed it would be George at work. He squeezed through the gateway and followed the broken-tile path where a line of weatherworn, stone troughs bordered the way, spilling out surviving masses of primroses, sadly half-choked by chickweed. Passing the old bike, fossilized to the shack of a shed, he discovered that the sound of industry was coming from behind the walls that enclosed the back yard. The conglomeration of tools and implements cluttered every inch of available space. Amidst the huddle of junk and ironmongery, the variety of cats lay sleeping in their chosen hideaways and were oblivious to all and sundry. Guy gazed at the handsome tiger-like specimen on the wall, wondering if this sleek length of fur was the randy Willie.

Guy peered over the wall and there, sure enough, was George shooting out the odd spark as he hammered iron on iron. He seemed to be hellbent on straightening the prongs of a garden fork and Guy could only marvel as the aged sinewy arm struck resoundingly on target until the prongs were to his satisfaction. The hammering ceased.

"Good morning, George! So, this is what you get up to?"

"What the..." he snarled aggressively, raising himself up, hammer in hand. Gradual recognition replaced the barbed-wire grimace to a smile as he squinted up through the thick lenses of his spectacles. "Oh, it's you, sir! For a moment, I thought…well, I'm not used to callers – but seeing as it's you here - Good-day to you, sir!" He touched his tattered old cap.

"Sorry, George, I didn't mean to startle you, sorry about that. You look fine and busy…"

"Aye! I've plenty to do."

"Well I haven't come to bother you. It's just that I lost my appetite at lunchtime so I though your cats would finish off these salmon sandwiches."

"Cats finish 'em off!? I'll finish 'em off meself!" George snatched the sandwiches as Guy handed them over the wall. "If you don't mind, sir, I'll be having these for me tea! What a treat! I was always partial to a tasty bit of salmon as ma' old mother would tell you. Oh yes, far too good for moggies! They'd never touch another mouse if they got their whiskers into a nice bit of salmon!"

"That's fine with me, George – you go ahead and have them for your tea."

"Thank you kindly, sir. Now then, are you going to join me with a drop of me best parsnip wine? I've nowt else to offer you."

"That's alright, George. I haven't come to hold you up. I just came along for the walk and to bring you the sandwiches."

"Oh, you're not holding me up, sir! I've all day and me time's me own! I'll have to open you the yard gate; I keep it barred – you never know who's about these days, do you?" He picked his way through the jungle of junk, then heaved away with an amazing amount of Herculean strength until the heavy iron bar was removed from the gate. "This way, sir, if you can find your way through all the trappings."

Guy battled through a bizarre maze of piled-up scrap-metals; skeleton-parts of rust encrusted engines, numerous oil cans, rolls of wire, terracotta pots, lengths of rope, brushes, spars, bars, barrels and boxes before he reached the back-door where the old fellow was beckoning him into the dark interior of a kitchen, which seemed to be little more than a covered extension of the back-yard. The stench of cat-faeces from within was something that Guy had never encountered in his whole life. The revolting resurgence of it hit him like a wall as he entered. Old George, being conditioned to the pong, was unaware of his visitor's discomfort and promptly dusted a couple of cats from the cushion of a rush-seated rocking-chair.

"Well, sit y'self down here on ma' mothers chair. This was where she always did her knitting. Said she'd nursed and fed me as a baby on this chair, and I know she would never have objected to a gentleman and a scholar like yourself, sir, sitting there."

"Thanks, George" Guy said, wishing he'd been offered a gas mask instead.

"Now then, I'll just pop these sandwiches out of the moggies' way and then we'll be having a drop of me best wine." He moved to an odd arrangement of cupboards, which took up most of the wall, then he placed the sandwiches inside before removing a large, corked bottle of wine.

Blowing the dust from two stemmed wineglasses, he carried them and the bottle over to the dish-drainer at the stone sink, where it took him several minutes to remove the cork. Guy, still wanting to come up for air, could only sit and stare at his antics, and more so at the considerable amount of clutter in the place. The whole room was reminiscent of a scrapyard, though not as tidy.

40

Covered with a frayed and tattered bit of heavily stained oil-cloth, the central oak table with its matching balloon-back chairs must have been worth a small fortune but, in George's book, was merely there to support his bevy of rusty tools, pots and pans, crate of milk, half-opened tins of cat food and a stack of galvanised buckets. To the actor's added amazement there was even an old wooden wheelbarrow and spade stuck in one corner of the room.

"Here you are, sir. I doubt it will taste as good as your Scotch whiskey, but it'll certainly set your whiskers on fire just the same!"

"Thanks, George." Guy raised the glass aloft. "And before we go any further, I must insist on you calling me Guy. You know me well enough by now to call me by my name, okay?"

"Okay, I'll call you Guy, sir"

"Good lad, cheers!"

"Cheers it is, sir!"

With an evening performance to come, Guy would normally have refused any kind of wine in the middle of the afternoon, but he needed something to offset the fetid atmosphere of the kitchen.

"It looks a good colour. Wouldn't know it from whiskey, George!" He took a quick gulp of the parsnip wine and almost shot off his seat. "Wow, George! What a kick!"

The old chap's grin stretched from wizened ear to wizened ear, giving him the appearance of a chimpanzee. "Told you it would set your whiskers on fire, didn't I?"

"How the devil d'you get a result like that from parsnips?"

"Good *fermertation"* he mispronounced with the utmost pride, removing his cap to dust away a cat from where he was about to sit.

"How old is the wine then, George?"

"Now you're asking me. It's getting on a bit, like me. Must be ten years since I made it, if it's a day!"

Guy almost choked over his next sip. "You mean, this stuff's ten years old?"

"It's got to be at least that! I haven't had any parsnips in the ground for donkey's years, so I suppose you could say it was time it was getting supped. Drink up and I'll pour you another one."

"No, I mustn't have anymore, George. I'm on the stage tonight!"

"It's not quite the season for fishing, sir!"

"Fishing?"

"If you're thinking of using the landing-stage up at Yonder Pool, I should think again. It's as rotten as a cart-load of muck! I'd fish from the bank if I were you, sir!"

"I'm not going fishing, George. When I say I'm going on-stage – I'm referring to the theatre."

"Theatre? I've never been to the theatre in ma' life! Never been anywhere except when I had to go off to the war."

"Yes, you told me about being in the war, George."

"Did I?"

"Yes, when we had the scotch together. Remember you were telling me about Mary, who'd lived up there during the war years?"

"So I was! And now you've come to mention it, sir, I *did* find something in ma' mothers belongings that you might care to see – it's an old snapshot of that young couple from April Cottage. Taken in happier days.

"Really, George!?" Guy was on his feet with enthusiasm. "Oh, I'd like to see that! Could you find it for me?"

"Of course, I can put me hand right on it, but I'll do it presently. Just sit yourself down again and finish your drink, so that I can top it up for you again."

The rush-seated rocker squeaked as Guy sat down again. All he could think about was getting his hands on that photograph. The thought of actually seeing Mary and her husband excited him beyond anything. It was something tangible to latch onto. He drank the wine to hasten the opportunity of seeing it.

"Four pounds of parsnips to the gallon with three pounds of sugar – that's the secret!" The old man was moving towards him again with the bottle. "And a good squirt of lemon!"

"It's truly excellent, George, but I mustn't have any more" Guy said, covering the top of his glass with his hand.

"Away with you, sir! We've only just started. This won't hurt you – a child could drink it! I've drank many a tumbler of this when I was a lad!"

"Then you're used to it, George! I'd say this stuff was ten times more potent than whiskey!" Guy was already feeling the effects of the half-glass he'd drunk and now he was being almost threatened to take more. He allowed the glass to be topped up.

"Now then..." Old George shuffled over to his chair and plonked himself down with a grin. "Here's to you, sir! A gentleman...and a scholar!"

"Thanks, George! Good health!"

41

During the next hour, the perceptions of his Gloucestershire upbringing, concerning those most genteel of country pursuits, had been effectively blown away with the sound of the hunter's horn. Guy was now wise to the very real rustics of country life, having been enlightened about everything from rabbiting with ferrets, to tickling trout in a woodland stream. George Smith esquire had rattled on for almost an hour, giving his newfound friend no alternative but to submissively bask, like the cats, on the rush-seat armchair, contented to be carried into the pasturelands of the old man's memory.

Strangely enough, the stench of cat-urine had diffused itself into oblivion and what is more, amidst all the extraordinary clutter in George's kitchen, Guy was beginning to be as comfortable as the proverbial old shoe. Too comfortable! With an increasing sense of befuddlement, his glazed expression had seen the frequent approach of the wine bottle with the old man's tilting hand topping his glass until the level of wine in the bottle had dropped dramatically.

"George…" Guy muttered eventually, wondering why the room went on rocking when his chair wasn't. "I do think it's time I made a move. I have to be at the theatre by seven." He managed to get onto his feet. Feet that didn't seem to be his own. George rose at the same time but didn't seem to be having any problem with his feet.

"Well, sir, I must say how much I've enjoyed your company; it's many a long year since a neighbour from April Cottage has dropped in. Oh yes, and that reminds me – the snapshot from ma' mother's belongings! I'll just get it for you, sir, if you'll hang on a jiffy?"

Guy hung on alright; to anything he could grab hold of. He edged along the side of the table, half-stumbling over the curled bit of matting where one of the cats was sharpening its claws.

"Mind yourself little pussy-puss!" He grinned inanely at the unfortunate animal who was too slow to avoid having a clumsy foot brought heavily down on its tail. The pitiful thing shot under the table with a piercing shriek just as Guy inadvertently knocked a galvanised bucket from the table, bringing it clattering to the floor where it rolled to a standstill by the open back-door. "whoops, puss! Look what you've done now!"

He hovered over the bucket at the doorway before giving it a wobbly kick into the yard where it rolled to join the rest of the junk. "I've just kicked the bucket!" he declared to himself, with a silly smile and a hiccough, as the fresh air hit him like a bullet.

"Here we are, sir, I've managed to find it." George's voice droned from behind.

"I've kicked the bucket, George!" Guy slurred with an impish grin.

"And what bucket is that, sir?"

"What bucket, George? Don't be shh – silly, George!" Guy said, turning to give George a ridiculously juvenile expression. "That bucket, there by the *shtirrupp plump* – the syrup stump – I'll get it in a minute, George…" He burst into convulsive laughter and the old man finally realised that his gentleman visitor was more than slightly tipsy.

"Oh dear, sir! I think you've been having a drop too much of ma' parsnip wine!"

"I think I have, George!" he hiccoughed again, wandering precariously into the middle of the yard, sprawling over a roll of wire netting and landing himself into the middle of a large motor tyre.

"On your feet, sir, that's it. Now let me help you to the gate. Mind yourself now and take it steady."

APRIL COTTAGE

Guy allowed himself to be manoeuvred in and out of the junk, along the broken-tiled path towards the arched gateway in the yard wall.

"Will you be alright, sir? Perhaps I'd best go along with you along the lane?"

"No, I'll be fine, George. I know my way." Guy grinned, stumbling out onto the lane staring confusedly into the wrong direction.

"It's that way, sir" George indicated.

"So it is, *Sheorge!*" Guy said with a stupefied smile. "Well, *Sheerio* and thank you again, old mate! Thank you for your kind *hospi…hospittletality…*"

"Take this with you, sir!" The old man pushed a scruffy brown envelope into the pocket of Guy's jacket. "that old snapshot is of no use to me. Its rightful place is at April Cottage – and many thanks for calling, sir! I shall be looking forward to that bit of salmon for ma' tea!"

George stood watching Guy ambling unsteadily away towards the bend in the lane, waiting with more than a little concern until his visitor was out of sight, then knotting the fringed string around the gatepost, he muttered to himself approvingly "Aye! A real gentleman, that one!" His face creased into that monkey-like grin. "He enjoyed that drop of ma' best parsnip wine! Aye, he did that! Make no mistake!" With that, George moved slowly towards the back-yard where he picked up his hammer once again.

42

The afternoon sunshine arched down over a proscenium of pink blossom shedding cruel lighting onto a crestfallen matinee idol. The apple tree's gnarled old trunk was Guy's only prop as he wretchedly spewed out an evil stream of parsnip wine froth. An unfortunate patch of sprouting young daffodils were on the receiving end. Through glazed helpless eyes he watched another shower of glistening globules shooting uncontrollably from his mouth, giving the poor daffodils another pasting of regurgitated wine. He wondered what it would kill first – them or him?

He had no recollection of how he'd made it back along the lane or how he'd coped with the five stone steps up to the cottage. Instead, his whole life seemed to be flashing before him as his erupting stomach continued to reject its contents. If there was an opposite to an orgasm – this was it! "Never, never again!" he scowled, as another fountain of venomous fluid spurted forth. "Never again, you blasted idiot!".

"Please, no more!" he whispered into the trunk of the supportive old tree. For what seemed an eternity, he leaned against it before floundering his way into the cottage and slumping agonizingly onto the sofa. His eyes managed to focus onto his watch; it was almost four-fifteen. He groaned into the cushion. Just over three hours to curtain-up. *How in God's name am I going to make it?* He turned onto his back, gazing up at a cobweb in the corner of the white-washed ceiling. *I shall have to ring 'Bron and tell him that I'm too ill to go on. Sod it – I can't do that; he'll have a heart attack!* Things had been bad enough this morning when Dee had talked of walking-out. *I've got to make it somehow,* he thought, feeling totally disgusted with himself. There was only one other time when Guy had allowed this kind of thing to happen. It was years ago after one of Roxanne's lunch-time cocktail do's, when all and sundry had been invited, including a colourful band of Mexican dancers who's brought along a case of tequila or two. They'd almost had to carry him on-stage that night, and it had been a nightmarish experience he'd sworn never to repeat.

He'd crawled from the sofa to the kitchen-sink and turned on the single tap. The icy water gushed out with such force that it bounced onto the stone surface of the sink, spurting all over his face and sweater. Cursing, he reduced the flow and despite the objections of his entire system, he forced two or three glassfuls of water down his throat. It was the only cure he knew. It had worked before and it was going to have to work again, and soon, he told himself as he stumbled through the kitchen towards the sitting-room's telephone.

"Hello there? Theatre Royal, back stage? Yep, get me Mr. Mercer please. Never mind who's calling! Just get him! And I don't much like your attitude either! No, I'm not the press, the name's Anderson! Now will you get me Oberon Mercer!?" Guy, satisfied that he'd finally got through to the idiot on the other end of the line, flopped down into the deep-seated armchair, staring down, once more, over the dinginess of the faded carpet. *Come on...COME ON!* He seethed with mounting impatience.

"Oberon Mercer, at your request?"
"About time, 'Bron. Where've you been?"
"Well I..."
"Okay, okay...I don't want your life history, I want a quick word before I do a Rip-Van-Winkle on you! Now just listen, and try not to interrupt! I'm having a slight problem; yes - another one! Don't interrupt – I'm a dying man! I've been a silly boy, 'Bron. Called on a neighbour who insisted on filling my glass with his homemade wine. Potent as hell! It's nearly killed me! I'm

going to be fine – that is, as long as you do what I ask you to do..." Oberon, fearing the worst managed to retain some degree of calm and agreed to take heed. Guy sighed gratefully. "Right, I want you to arrange a taxi to pick me up here at six forty-five, prompt! No, I'm not incapable of driving – just got enough alcohol in my blood to excite the entire local constabulary! Stop doing your good-fairy act and listen! Yes, I know what I'm doing – I've brought most of the stuff up and I've consumed a couple of pints of *Adam's Ale*. Now I need to get some shut-eye for at least an hour; to sleep it off. Request number two is an alarm-call from you, otherwise I shall sleep forever. I need you to give me a call at six-fifteen? That will give me enough time to get ready before the taxi arrives!"

"But..."

"Ill, be there, 'Bron!" Guy interrupted. "You just make sure the taxi gets here on time and don't forget to give him directions; it's a bit off the beaten track – and remember, an alarm call at six-fifteen! It's got a very loud ring. Thanks, 'Bron – I won't let you down – and I suggest you keep it to yourself, otherwise my name will be mud again!"

After labouredly attempting to replace the telephone onto the nearby table, Guy made a fruitless attempt to raise himself from the cosy depths of the old armchair. It was akin to raising the dead as his mind became inert and his body began responding to the quiet contentment of the surroundings. His eyelids closed to screen out the razzle-dazzle of sunbeams on the window's latticed panes. It was then that he sensed the cool, comforting hand on his brow, blotting out the pain; gently and lovingly pressurizing until it seemed to touch his very soul. He had neither the will, nor the inclination to do anything but submit to the strong presence within the room.

43

The show went on. Guy was too much of a professional to shirk his responsibilities to either the theatre-going public or his fellow actors. Despite the effects of the hangover, he managed to give Trevor Adams all the panache and style necessary to excite his audience; and to once again satisfy the demands of Delia's Vanda, who was played with more than the usual ardour; certainly, that possessive kiss at the end of the play expressed her feelings of euphoria very clearly indeed.

Dutifully satisfied with the performance's sustained, final applause, Guy fled from the stage to the sanctity of his dressing-room. Closing the door behind him he plonked himself onto the plastic chair to stare disdainfully at his tired, grease-paint image in the harshness of the neon-lit mirror. It was a grim face that stared back at him. Wearily, he began to cream away the make-up from where the continued pain throbbed on relentlessly. What was uppermost in his mind now was to get away from the theatre, and civilisation, as quickly as he could. He'd arranged for the taxi to pick him up at the stage-door at ten forty-five. He had ten minutes left and wished it was less; such was his eagerness to return to the solitude of April Cottage. Despite its air of foreboding and presentiment, there was a distinctive peace there ready to welcome him into its timeless cocoon.

44

Suddenly, there came a knocking on the dressing-room door, causing Guy to snap out of his solitary peace. He chose to ignore it, but the knocking continued with a maddening resonance.

"Go away!" he called, with a facial expression that threatened to kill. For a merciful moment, it seemed that whoever it was had gone. Several seconds later, the knocking continued, though now it was more of a gentle tapping. "Well, don't just stand there knocking! Either come in or piss off!" It wouldn't have made any difference if it had been the Queen! There was a short pause before the door slowly opened with a nervously excitable female voice quivering from behind it.

"Sorry to bother you, Mr. Anderson – but I'd be over-the-moon if you would just sign this photo of yourself for me?" The door opened a little wider and the voice grew a little bolder. "My name is Lorna – I'm a member of the staff here at the theatre. I wouldn't usually bother you like this, but I've been trying to catch you ever since you came here, duck. I hope you don't mind my intrusion to your private room, but I do so desperately want your autograph and the chance to say hello. Anyone will tell you, duck, that Lorna from the box-office is your biggest fan!"

She was big alright. He turned to face the sheer bulkiness of a middle-aged woman almost wedged in the doorway. She stood beaming at him; unabashed and rosy-faced with a pen poised over one of his latest glossy publicity folders, which incidentally, he loathed.

So, this was the lady that Oberon had warned him about. *Okay, 'Bron, you win!* Taking the folder from her willing hands, he wandered over to sit at the dressing table.

"Oh, thank you, duck…thank you!" she wobbled in breathlessly and stood over him like a tank. "I can't tell you how much I've wanted to meet you. I've worshipped you from afar. Never thought I'd be this close to you!"

"What did you say your name was?"

"It's Lorna!" she gulped, as she watched her hero inscribing his famous name over her prized photograph.

"There you go then, Lorna…" He smiled, handing her the folder.

"Oh, thank you very much indeed, Mr. Anderson! You're the best! You really are!"

There were tiny beads of sweat standing out on her broad nose and dimpled cheeks as she took it from him with an almost profound reverence.

"Now then, Lorna, I have to go, so…"

"I can't believe it, getting this! And you've written my name above yours! Oh, thank you so much! Wait until my friend sees this – she's in the post-office you know – chief cashier! We've been friends for years; both widows now – but merry ones! No point in there being anything else is there, duck?"

"No, Lorna" he said, escorting her to the door. "forgive me now, will you, but I've got a taxi coming anytime. I have to dash."

"Yes, and I've got to get up to the bus station; last bus goes at eleven – and when I get home, this is going straight on the side-board in a frame. I'll put it next to my old man's picture!" She cackled with laughter as he ushered her into the passage. "Don't forget, duck, look in when you pass the box-office, I'm there every night! God bless you for this!" She kissed the folder and winked in Guy's direction.

Guy was about to close the door behind Lorna but was utterly irritated to see that Dee had suddenly made an appearance behind his departing visitor. She was making it quite plain that her way was blocked.

"Excuse me, do you think I could come through, please?"

"Oh, I'm sorry, duck!" Lorna responded, immediately recognising the leading-lady. The large, but lovable Lorna breathed in, allowing the haughty actress to squeeze through and to make her pretentious entrance into Guy's dressing room. Lorna couldn't fail to see Guy's irritable expression at this intrusion and she laid a comforting, chubby hand on his shoulder. "Don't stand any nonsense, duck! Tell her what you told me – you've got a taxi to catch" she whispered in his ear.

Guy leant in and quietly spoke confidingly "between you and me, Lorna, there're those who can take a hint and those who can't!"

"Say no more, duck, say no more!" Her laughter echoed as she wobbled off down the corridor.

45

No sooner than Guy had closed the dressing-room door, Dee's whining began.

"And who in God's name was that!? Yet another adoring fan?" Dee was sitting at his dressing-room mirror. Guy began gathering his belongings together in an effort to show her he was hurrying.

"Look, Dee, this is the wrong time for a chat – I've got a thumping headache and I need to get back!"

"I know that! That's why I'm here!" She began twirling bits of her fringe in the mirror.

"What do you mean – that's why you're here?" He switched off the dressing-table lights in sheer annoyance. "I've got a taxi waiting outside!"

"No, you haven't" she said, calmly rising to face him. "I've sent him away!"

"You did what!?" Now, Guy was fuming with rage.

"You don't need a taxi, Guy, darling, because I'm going to run you back!"

"Oh, no you're not! No way! You can go back right now and re-order that taxi for me! I mean it!"

"I'm sorry, Guy, but I'm going to have to insist on taking you back. It's perfectly clear to me that you're not well and you need someone to care for you. Look at you – there's not a bit of colour in your cheeks, you look decidedly sallow! Your eyes are as bloodshot as hell, darling!"

"It's nothing more than a hangover and I need sleep. Damnit all, woman! I can't believe you've sent my taxi away! Whatever possessed you to do a crazy thing like that?" Guy's temples were pounding and the hostility in his glare increased. "Don't think that you can go around organising my life for me, because you can't! Do you hear? I've done with all of that kind of thing! I don't want any woman planning my life; giving me motherly advice, changing my unhealthy habits, ruining my well-laid plans and turning away my taxi-cabs! Is that plain enough for you? Perhaps you'll go home now and leave me to re-arrange a taxi-ride home!" He stormed over to the door. Dee got to the door before him, barring his way and holding onto him, scared out of her wits that she might lose him.

"Please, Guy, listen to me! I'm only thinking of you, I swear it!" Her hands moved to his face. "I really didn't think you would mind if I ran you home. I thought you'd be pleased. I thought we had an understanding?" Her fingers were stroking his hair. "Let me run you home, just this once? Please, Guy?"

"And what then?" he asked with sardonic expression. "What happens next? Do you intend to return to the hotel?"

"Well that's up to you, Guy. Whatever you like?"

"Haven't I made it plain what I'd like? If I haven't, let me rephrase it! I require solitary confinement of the highest order! Precisely that and nothing else, Dee darling!"

She made a weak effort to protest but she could feel the pressure of his hands on her shoulders as he stressed his point home.

"It's no use, my lovely Delia – I've reached a stage in my life where I don't need anyone to look after me. I'm perfectly capable of doing that myself!"

"Oh, is that right!?" she said with a sudden burst of sarcastic aggression. "Well isn't that just fine and dandy for you!? Well, let me tell you that I'm absolutely sick of looking after *my*self, sick of it! Do you hear!?" Her green eyes were suddenly very tearful and she moved away from him, hastily searching through her bag for a cigarette. "Every single night after the performance, I climb into an empty hotel bed – whether it be Scarborough,

Birmingham, Glasgow, now in Stoke-on-Trent, and soon in the Great Metropolis! Wherever I go, it's the same story; an empty bed with cold sheets and a single pillow!" Guy watched as she lit the cigarette. "It's easier for a man to be his own person – and before you say that 'women have never had it so good' – this particular woman thinks we've never had it so bad! All we've got out of this damned equality is a lack of courtesy and much less respect from you so-called gentlemen!" She sat on the dressing-table chair again. "Perhaps I shouldn't be in the theatre at all!" She blew a cloud of smoke into the air, following it with a troubled gaze. "I gave up everything I had for acting!" She removed her spectacles and dabbed her eyes with a scrappy bit of tissue before turning herself a more than critical examination in the dressing-table mirror. "Now look at me! Well-past my sell-by-date! No wonder the great Guy Anderson doesn't fancy me – who would!?"

"Rubbish, Dee! You're a lovely woman and you know it! You're still young, too!" Guy knew that it was well within his power to take this woman in his arms and make her completely happy. He'd had the proof of that only hours ago when he'd gone into her room.

He'd had to dodge women like Dee Davidson all of his life, even during his happier years with Roxanne. It was the price of being put on a pedestal. *Price?* He supposed that many men would consider it to be more of a prize! A few years ago, he would have readily agreed with them, but now, after almost five glorious decades, he was beginning to prefer the adoration without the involvement. Guy's biggest problem was that he'd already allowed himself to get foolishly involved with this fifty-year-old femme fatale and now, like a fool again, seeing her depressed state as she leaned over the pots of stage make-up, he knew that he was about to submit yet again. His adoring co-star was suddenly a frail and tragic figure. So utterly vulnerable. Where was her controlled poise and glamour now? Or was this just another performance?

It was no act! Dee was staring at an ashen-faced reflection of herself with the tiny wisps of smoke filtering into a pair of screwed-up, despairing eyes. She never allowed herself to indulge in desperation for long; she was good at readdressing herself and the actress within was then quick to take over. Giving her image a reprimanding glance, she turned sharply away from the mirror and dramatically stubbed her cigarette onto an ashtray.

"You know what you are, don't you, Guy? You're a shit!"

He barred her way as she made for the door. "Dee…"

"Nothing but a shit! Get out of my way!"

"Listen…"

"I don't want to listen. The quicker I get away from you, the better! I'm going to drive myself back to the hotel as I should have done straight after the performance. Goodnight, Guy!"

"What about me" he asked, provokingly. "You've sent my taxi home!"

"I don't give a shit!"

"Don't keep saying that" he chided. "It's not lady-like."

"Why should I be a lady? There are clearly no gentlemen around here! Now get out of my way!"

As she tried to pass him, he caught hold of her wrists, forcing her face-to-face with his taunting expression. "But didn't you say *you* were going to run me back to the cottage?"

There was an almighty silence before she finally submitted.

"You bastard!" she whispered.

46

"Well, if this is it, it's just about ten times worse than I thought it was going to be!" Dee exclaimed as she walked into the dimly lit kitchen of April Cottage and slammed her car keys down onto the scrubbed table. Guy was well-prepared for her reaction.

"What you see is what you get! Don't say I didn't warn you – you might as well make yourself at home; that is, if you're thinking of staying?"

"Well if it wasn't for the fact that I'd need a navigator to get me back to Stoke-on-Trent, no-one would persuade me to stay here, not even you, Guy Anderson! I couldn't face those eerie lanes on my own, I'd be scared of meeting something or indeed *someone* on those creepy bends!"

"Yep – it's a right old squeeze with the Jag." He jabbed at the dead embers in the grate with a poker. "But then, you rarely meet anything up here."

"Not surprised! Who else would want to come along here to this dump? Now I can understand why that girl called here when she had a puncture – she must have been terrified out on that lane, at that time of night!"

"She was!" Guy hid his guilty expression in the grate, adding a few sticks to the fire and hoping that he would continue to get away with the deceit. "But she was okay again when I'd fixed her up."

"What on earth possesses you, Guy, to come to a place like this? Just look at it! It's an abysmal little hovel!"

"I like it, Dee – simple as that! Did you ever read 'Children of the New Forest?'"

"Read it? I've not even heard of it!"

"It's just one of those books we had to read in school. It made some impression on me, I suppose. I sort of connect it with this place. I don't know why? Strange really, because I couldn't tell you what the book's about; there must be some association in the narrative, I should think. It's probably lying dormant in my subconscious."

"There's more than that lying dormant, Guy! I really can't come to terms with the fact that you actually like it here. You could choose anything. Anything! The most desirable country residence with style and all *mod cons*...and you choose this hovel? Why? It's so cold here! It must be so bad for you!" She lit a cigarette and moved nearer to the fireplace.

"You choose to smoke – why? Because you like it? I think smoking is very bad for you, but you still smoke because you get something out of it."

"Point taken. Shall we have some coffee?"

"Sorry, Dee – I don't think I should build the fire up too much at this time of night; it's a bit dangerous to leave if we're going to retire, so I can't boil the fire-kettle."

"So, use the electric kettle!"

"There isn't one. Can I interest you in a glass of milk or a drop of wine? Something that will make you sleep?"

She gave him an incredulous look.

"Well don't just stand there with your mouth open, Dee! I didn't exactly invite you to come here, did I? And this is precisely why! I knew this wouldn't be your scene!"

"You're damned right, it isn't! It's not surprising that you've been looking so peaky lately. This place is enough to kill anyone off. There's about as much warmth in here as there is in a funeral parlour!"

"Oh, but Dee, it's so wonderful when the fire's lit, as you will see when you come down for breakfast. We'll have hot, buttered toast like you've never tasted before – but, for now, Dee, I really must get some shut-eye if I ever want to get rid of this damned hangover. I suggest we go and snuggle down together, unless you'd like to have a wander round first?"

"Wander round? Are you mad?"

"I thought you might like to inspect the other rooms before we retire?" he said with a provoking gleam in his eye.

"No, thank you – not if this one's anything to go by! Just the bathroom, please – and I dread to think what that's like!"

"Well it's not up to your style; very basic indeed, but it's clean. I'll show you. Come on." He settled the small fire down and switched off the light as they went through to the tiny passage at the foot of the stairs.

"What's through there?" Dee asked, pointing towards the sitting-room door.

"Nothing much – just another small room." Guy tried to sound casual, silently praying that the time for any strange sounds or psychic activity was not now! At that moment in time, all he wanted was to fall into the deepest of deep sleeps, which would finally diminish the dull pain in his head.

"Let me have a look then?" Dee was obviously curious to see the room. He had no alternative but to open the door.

"Again, it's very basic, as you can see. I only come in here to use the phone."

Dee gave the room a stony glance. "Shut the door, I've seen enough! Is the bathroom upstairs?"

"Yep – and mind how you go up the stairs, they're rather steep!"

Dee's face was a picture when she saw the bathroom. The cramped little room with its low sloping roof was indescribably primitive; a distinctly still-life study in murky-white; comprising a poky hand-bowl with a squat little lavatory basin and a grim-looking iron bath with pedestal feet.

"The emersion heater's on if you wish to take a dip?"

"I wouldn't feel clean if I took a dip in that! I'd rather take a dip in a rain-tub!"

"Well there's one in the back-yard if you're so inclined?" he quipped, moving into the bedroom and removing his jacket. She followed him in with a sullen expression, frowning around the faded rose-papered walls, taking in the rest with equal disdain. The drab, curtained wardrobe in the corner, the nondescript black-framed pictures over the chest of drawers, the tiny dormer-window and finally the bed. The bed was a hideous oak antiquity covered with bulky blankets and a faded fringed coverlet. To Guy, it was merely somewhere to lay his aching limbs and he dispensed with every unnecessary preliminary in order to get there.

"Aren't you having a wash?" she asked.

"In the morning."

"You're not getting into bed with your shirt on! Where are your pyjamas?"

"You can wear them if you like?" he said, making sure there was enough weariness in his voice to prevent her expecting any miracles. "They're in the top drawer." He gave an exaggerated yawn and his head hit the pillow.

Dee simply hadn't been prepared for any of this. Certainly not such a decisive display of 'not tonight, Josephine!' – it was going to take something more than faith to move this mountain. She stood rather forlornly, looking down over his immovable shape beneath the bedclothes and felt like an intruder.

"Guy?" she eventually uttered after a long, cold wait of silence.

"Hmm?"

"Are you going to sleep?"

"Hmm?"

"I presume that means that you're actually going to sleep!?"

"Hmm?"

"FINE!" She reacted with a vocal projection fit for the back-stalls. "I hope you have a bloody good night!"

Guy answered with a short, contrived snore.

Dee stormed into the bathroom, mainly to relieve herself. She squatted over the toilet basin, keeping her distance from the revolting plastic seat, attempting to aim straight. Afterwards, the wait for the hot water to run into the dingy little hand-bowl seemed indeterminable. Guy's soap, towel and toothbrush were there and she took advantage of these for a hasty brush-and-swill before venturing back into the cold bedroom. Guy hadn't moved and was well on the way to dreamland. She wanted to scream her frustrations to the rafters, but instead found some solace in lighting another cigarette.

Dee didn't know whether she felt rejected, or merely ridiculous. In that moment, she didn't know whether she loved or loathed that immovable lump in the bed. She'd been so certain of everything, expecting to go on from where they'd left off that morning. In view of his own little short-coming he could have at least allowed her to make love to him, until he fell asleep in her arms as she'd promised. She knew nothing of the parsnip-wine episode, putting his hangover down to an over-indulgence in his beloved Beaujolais. Surely, by now, he should have learned to cope with a drop or two of his favourite wine. It was just no excuse for the objectionable behaviour he was now subjecting her to. If only she hadn't cancelled that taxi-cab! She would now be warm and cosy in her hotel room with the rest of the cast. For once, she envied them all for being so sensible.

She moved around to Guy's side of the bed and stared down at him. His face was peeping out from the top-sheet with the white fold skimming his dark moustache and half-opened mouth. She leaned over him until she could feel his steady breathing on her face. She wanted to kiss the dark lashes fringing his closed eyelids. God, he was so handsome, even in that semi-conscious state! The slumbering portrayal of boyish innocence made her feel infinitely protective and privileged – just to be there with him.

She did love him! She really loved him! She pushed back the stray wisps of hair from his brow and stroked her fingers through the rest of his hair, then putting beside all of her own desires, she realized that he needed that sleep far more than he needed her.

47

With her clothes removed, Dee was shivering violently. She couldn't get his navy, initialled pyjamas on quick enough. She struggled into them and they were ridiculously long on her petit frame. This certainly wasn't how she'd planned things when she'd cancelled the taxi; this was to be a sequel to the exciting preview she'd taken part in earlier. This was to have been an evening of allurement with a tantalizing strip-show that would have had them both ending up starkers between the sheets. Even she had to see the funny side now, as she stood in the oversized pyjamas, feeling like a ludicrous penguin in that distant little bedroom. She moved to her side of the bed, struggling with the extra length of the trouser-bottoms cluttering around her ankles. Dee half-climbed into the bed before realising she hadn't switched the light off. Despite her inertia it had to go off; there was no way she was going to get any sleep if she had to stare at the bloody-awful wallpaper. Sleep was going to be difficult enough. Off went the light and she struggled through the

APRIL COTTAGE

chill and darkness to climb into his desirable warmth.

Guy was turned with his back to her but she snuggled up closely; her feet touching his and her free hand moving down over his shirt to rest on the firmness of his thigh. For the time being, his lack of response didn't matter; she was there with him, sharing his bed and that was the important thing. It was a whole flight of steps in the right direction. Sleeping with this man was everything she'd dreamed of since their eyes had first met. Her palms stroked against the tautness of his lower limbs and her body moved in closer and closer, as she prepared herself for what she suspected was going to be a sleepless vigil. In the silence of that dowdy little room, she lay listening to his steady breathing and was reminded of Ralph. Her estranged husband's breathing was anything but steady due to his adenoidal problems. She still thought of him with affection and hoped that he was happy with Wendy; God knows the two of them deserved some happiness after what she'd done to them.

48

Wendy and Ralph had been a pair long before Dee had arrived on the scene. She winced, recalling the way she'd broken them up, merely to produce a marriage that was destined never to work. Ralph never did come to terms with Delia's theatrical career and the constant demands that it had made on their union. He did everything he could to bring her into the domesticity of their home, but the theatre was to take precedence over everything and it was soon plain that the two of them were never going to conform to each other's way of life. Even Clive, her only son, had sided with his father after the separation and she couldn't blame him! The poor boy had been undeniably affected by the demands of the theatrical touring – and in addition to being subjected to the constant arguments within the marriage, he'd been in and out of different schools for most of his childhood, and of course the whole thing had a devastating effect on his education.

Ralph had found all of this insufferable and it was too painful to recollect. Mercifully for all concerned, Wendy had been there waiting in the background with her ever-loving arms open wide. Wendy, in her wisdom, had undoubtedly foreseen it all ending the way it that it did. She was a very forgiving woman. Since then, Delia Davidson had thrown herself into her work and had sworn never to get herself involved with anyone else ever again.

That was until she'd met Guy Anderson.
She'd always had plenty of fantasies about him – *who hadn't?* Despite all her great theatrical aspirations, the thought of her ever working with him would have once seemed totally inconceivable. They'd first met, socially, two years ago – briefly, at a party – and then at a rather grand awards ceremony in London, where she'd considered herself privileged, thanks to a mutual agent, to be sharing the Anderson table with several other notables. She had been more than content to bask in the glory of being one of the unsuccessful nominees in a supporting role, while he, Guy Anderson, had predictably carried off the award for Best Actor. Roxanne had been there, bubbling over with more effervescence than the flowing champagne; anyone would have thought that it was she who had been up to collect the award. Over the tall cut glasses and massed flowers on the pink-clothed table, Dee had

watched the two of them like a hawk and her conclusions were that things in their relationship were not all they were cooked up to be. She'd heard the rumours and now it was plain to see; it was written all over that supremely handsome face. Roxanne was so blatantly over-the-top that she was a positive embarrassment to him. If it wasn't obvious to anyone else at the table, it was to Dee Davidson.

Then it happened – that totally unexpected moment over the direct diameter of the table, when she'd looked across to find his eyes riveted on her. It was a singular look of appraisal and he was actually mouthing words of congratulations to her regarding the nomination. From that moment, she'd set her sights on him; she was going to get as close to that personable, unassuming star of a man as was physically possible – and now, provocatively pressing herself against him as they lay secretly cocooned within the encompassment of the covers, she reckoned she wasn't doing too badly so far.

49

It was around three-in-the-morning when there came a hazy kind of light at the poky dormer window. Grey shadows shrouded the rest of the room and, after the sweet frustrations of longingly lying there, Dee had finally drifted off into a kind of semi-sleep, promising herself that the best was yet to come. Seconds later, she was painfully shocked into wakefulness by a violent blow to the face.

"Ow! What the hell was that!?" Her nose felt as if it had been flattened. It had certainly brought tears to her eyes and she couldn't work out what had happened. "Guy? Guy, what happened?"

It soon became clear that Guy was responsible for the blow. She could feel at once his trembling body and his arms were flailing about wildly. *Is he having some kind of fit?* Then he began calling out as though in great distress. *Is he having a nightmare?*

"Guy, wake up! You're having a bad dream! Wake up, darling!" Dee leaned across him and could feel the damp sweat on his shirt. She touched his face in an attempt to wake him, but his arms began lashing out again. She struggled to hold his wrists, realising that the nightmare must be horrendous.

"The wing's burning! Dear God, we're going down!" Guy's strangely muffled words were just clear enough for her to discern, but his ramblings were followed by a spate of indistinguishable mutterings hastening into a terrible, anguished cry, which was stifled into the pillow as he threw himself onto his stomach. It was then that his breathing seemed to stop and she felt his whole body stiffen against her.

Dee panicked through the stony silence that followed. She threw back the bedclothes, thinking he was having some kind of heart attack. The very thought of it made her cry out with distraught emotion.

"Please, Guy! Please wake up!"

50

After several terrifying minutes, Dee's fear was changed to instant relief, when she found that Guy was whimpering into his pillow like a child. She took him in her arms, cradling his head below her shoulder, retrieving the blankets with her free hand to gently cover him up again.

"*Shhh* – it's over now. You're here with me, darling." Guy's sobbing stopped almost instantly. He turned and leaned heavily against her and the subservience of having to bear his full weight gave her the most wondrous feeling; she wanted this moment to go on and on. "I will always be here for you, Guy. I love you so much!" She kissed him as she spoke, stroking his hair and touching his face with all the tenderness and love that was in her. Slowly he began to respond to the erotic movements of her body and after that sudden, spiritual involvement with a close-to-death experience, there was the pleasurable resurgence of new life stirring somewhere lower down in the bed. Dee was making sure of that!

51

"Breakfast is served, if madam would care to rise?" Guy called, in a deeply controlled voice from the bottom of the stairs. Dee responded with a long groan as he moved back into the glow of the kitchen fire to spear another round of bread. *She can sleep on if that's what she wants*, he thought, quite content to breakfast alone after having an early-morning walk along the lane.

He sipped hot tea, thinking about that ghastly nightmare; it was the worst he'd ever experienced. It had been such an intense, fearful dream that he wanted to obliterate it from his mind, but he knew it never would – it had been awesome enough to remain with him forever. Strangely, all he reflected about was death. His own death. It had all taken place in a past era.

With the comforting rays of morning light streaming in through the kitchen-room window, he tried to fathom out what could have motivated him to dream of piloting a doomed plane over wartime Germany. It must have been what old George had told him about the husband who, way back in the forties, had gone to war never to return, leaving a grieving young widow back here at April Cottage. *Of Course!* Guy conjectured, *that's why I had the dream!*

Guy stared at the piece of toast on the end of his fork. That wasn't the only motivation for the dream, *was it?* He had to admit to himself that it was all tied up with a number of other things relevant to him being there. From the very moment he'd arrived at the cottage, he'd been conscious of some shared affinity with the place. He was recounting those first feelings of déjà vu as he buttered his toast.

He began reflecting on the way that the extraneous intervention of an inner force had led him to the hidden grave in that bramble-covered corner of the little church-yard, and he'd been aware of it again in the sitting-room when he'd witnessed the transient, mystical figure of the woman, standing by the window. Through the timelessness of that empty room, he'd whispered to her with a voice that wasn't his own, urging her not to cry. The abrupt and uncanny silence that had followed signified that there had been a definite response to his plea. It was at that precise moment, as he took a bite of his toast, that he felt the lost pilot's existence manifesting itself deep within his own consciousness. That was the motivation.

APRIL COTTAGE

Last night, in the dream, he'd experienced it more acutely. When he'd dreamt of being there over Germany, he'd been at the controls. He'd seen the burning wing and heard the massive explosion that led to the final horrific moment when the bomber aircraft had crazily plummeted towards his violent death, and through the downward sweep of speeding clouds, he'd seen the illuminated face of a woman whose blonde hair was taken up at the sides with decorated clips. Her name had died on his lips as his plane, bursting into fateful flames, made contact with the alien gravity of German soil. Mercifully then, his head had hit the pillow.

The second piece of toast was charred to a cinder and there was something disturbingly symbolic about the smell of burning bread. Guy shook it off the end of the fork into the flames and speared another round, taking care not to burn it this time. He poured himself more tea and crunched into the toast, staring upwards towards the frame text over the mantelpiece.

PREPARE TO MEET THY GOD.

There was a meaningful significance there within the hanging oak frame with its illuminated lettering and staid ornamentation of lilies-of-the-valley. With that same inner compulsion, he rose from his seat to get a closer look. Growing curiosity drove him to remove it from the rusty hook on the wall. He blew the fragments of an ancient spider from the brown-paper backing and then saw a faded signature written in ink on the top left-hand corner. *Charles Barker.* Underneath, in pencil, someone had scrawled the words 'my great Grandfather'. Guy replaced the print rather quickly and drank more tea. Once again, he had been motivated to do something without any real explanation. *Weird!*

52

Repudiating it all as nonsense, Guy grabbed hold of his script. He needed to check on a small alteration in a section of scene-two. He found the place and read over it a few times, but then the lines became inconsequential compared with the inscriptions on the back of the print. He stared up once more at the framed text, realising that it must have belonged to the young Barkers; probably a family hand-me-down they'd received from a long-lost relative when they were first married – but if that were so, how had it managed to survive in the same spot when numerous tenants had been in and out of the property so many years after, especially since it was a rather gloomy-looking thing to have around?

Guy scanned the room, half-wishing that there were other things to find; other relics of the past that had perhaps belonged to the Barkers. If only there was something like a photograph - *A photograph!* He was on his feet, suddenly remembering that only yesterday, old George had given him one, or at least had promised to give him one. He vaguely remembered old George giving him something when he left Holly Cottage. *A snapshot! That's it! The old man called it a snapshot! My jacket-pocket!*

He heard noises coming from the room overhead and suspected that Dee had risen. He rushed to where his jacket draped the back of a chair and delved into the pockets. He drew out the scruffy brown envelope and took it over into the sunlight by the window. Holding the crumpled, grey snapshot, he gazed at the two, young people standing close together in the doorway of the cottage. They were both smiling, in a shy pose aimed at whoever was holding the camera. The man was in R. A. F. uniform and she was dressed like a typical forties-style housewife. Guy strained to see their faces more clearly but a surface crease on the photograph quickly put a stop to that. The man was obviously not much more than a youth and Guy noticed how neatly his wife fitted into the crook of his arm – and how proudly she was leaning against him – but most of all, he was struck by the undoubtedly familiarity of that girlish figure and the way that her blonde hair was brought up at the sides with clips. He knew, without a shadow of a doubt, that he was looking at the woman he'd seen by the sitting-room window; the woman he'd watched in the bedroom, holding the floral dress against the cheval mirror,

APRIL COTTAGE

and even more disturbingly; the woman he'd seen when staring through the clouds of last night's dream as his plane was spinning down to its death crash.

He knew that he was looking at a snapshot of Mary Ann Barker standing with her husband only yards away from where he was now standing himself. He turned it over to see the neat handwriting on the back: 'Us at April Cottage, 1941'.

There was something else inside that envelope. It appeared to be a crumpled piece of paper, which had been folded several times until it was almost falling apart. He unfolded it gently until the flimsy, creased squares were open and he could only stare blankly at the sombre black capitals of war-office officialdom:

APRIL COTTAGE

Regret to inform you
Flying-officer Edward Barker
Reported killed in action
October 19th, 1942

Guy muttered vacantly to himself as his fingers refolded the remnants of the telegram. His throat was dry, almost to the point of strangulation. His face was ashen as he questioningly mouthed the date. *October the nineteenth, nineteen forty-two!*

This was a day, month and year that was very personal to Guy.

Unbelievingly, this was *the* day, month and year of his birth.

53

The tiny bird hopping below the window on the gravel path offered him no answers. He watched it moving across the bit of patchy lawn towards the clump of a mole-hill, where it began pecking away at some poor, unsuspecting worm. Guy was deep in thought and jumped when the door burst open behind him. Dee, wearing his navy pyjamas and an unbelieving expression, burst in to stridently halt his train of analysis.

"Guy, this place is like a bloody shoe-box – and it looks even more depressing in the daylight! It's so cold; I'm perished! Is this bit of fire the only heat we've got in the place? My God, don't tell me that's the kitchen through there! Guy, look at me when I'm talking to you – I'm over here, not outside! Where's this delicious breakfast I'm supposed to be having? All I can smell is burnt toast!"

"Dee?" he said, turning from his window view and walking over to where she was standing, shivering by the fireplace. There was an uncomforting tone to his voice, which stopped her in her tracks as she waited for him to continue.

"…Do you believe in reincarnation?"

54

"What kind of a question is that?"

"Just give me a straight answer, yes or no?"

"No!" Dee shot the flippant reply into his ear, pressing a light kiss onto his bristly cheek. "Is that straight enough?"

"What *do* you believe in?

"I believe in love, darling. Love, sweet love!" She drawled, whilst her arms went up and around him. "What else would have brought me to an ice-box like this? Now, kiss me before I freeze to death!"

"I'm serious, Dee."

"So am I, darling. Deadly serious. Kiss me!"

"When you've answered the question! Do you believe in a person having had a past life?"

"I've told you, no! Now, kiss me!"

He kissed her quickly. "Why don't you believe in it?"

"What's all this, Guy? I haven't even had any breakfast yet; not even a cup of tea! And here you are going on about reincarnation! What's got into you?"

"Just tell me, please – why don't you believe in it?"

"Because I refuse to believe in anything like that!"

"Have you ever given it any thought?"

"Never! I'm a realist, Guy – and there's only one thing real to me at this moment – you and me! Now, is it too much to ask for a nice cup of tea? Jasmine, please..."

"Sorry, it's *English Breakfast* or nothing" Guy replied, replacing the kettle on the hob.

"Could I borrow your dressing-robe, please?"

"Sorry, I don't possess one, my dear – I'm not that kind of actor" Guy drawled, doing his best Noel Coward impersonation.

"I'll have to put something on before I go up those stairs again. When I got out of bed just now, I was rigid with cold! I couldn't face stripping off into my clothes and the water in the bath-room is only lukewarm."

"Sorry about that, Dee. I used it all up for my morning dip, but the immersion is on and it will soon warm up. Here, put this on for now..." He snatched the jacket from the back of the chair, dropping it onto her shoulders. She stood, hunched by the hearth watching in disbelief as he topped up the brown earthenware teapot with water.

"My God, I've seen everything now! That kettle is filthy, Guy! I'm surely not expected to drink the contents of that!?"

"Why not? It's only blackened on the outside. It's a fire kettle!"

"I can see that, darling" she snapped. "Anyway, I'm not that fussy about a drink – I'll have a cigarette instead."

"You smoke too much! Do you want toast?"

"I don't know…" she said, dubiously, as he held the short fork and a chunk of bread in readiness.

"Well, either you do or you don't? Please yourself!" The irritability in his voice alerted her to the fact that she was perhaps going a little too far.

"Go on then, I'll try a piece, please" she relented.

"I'm sorry about all this, darling, but I didn't exactly promise you the Ritz and jasmine tea, did I? You may find it hard to understand, but occasionally this is the way I like to live."

"Like camping-out, you mean?" Resignedly, she pulled up a wooden chair and watched as he proceeded to make toast over the glowing, red embers. His face, lit by the glow, was a picture of tranquillity. *He's really enjoying doing that*, she concluded to herself, *like a little boy with a new toy!* She let him play on, allowing him to pour her tea into the cup and butter her toast – it obviously gave him such delight that it would have been churlish of her to show any more resentment – and anyway, she reminded herself, she was well accustomed to playing the supporting role.

"Quite a pleasant change, this tea, Guy" she commented with a smile.

"Try the buttered toast while it's hot."

"Thanks, but it's oozing with butter. Very sinful!" She took a dainty bite.

"Well?" He waited, certain of her approval.

"Well…I must admit it's far nicer than those plastic triangles at the hotel. A bit of a smoky taste…not unpleasant though!"

"Have another?"

"Let me have a go – I've never toasted bread before over an open fire" she said with some degree of enthusiasm.

Guy was only too delighted to help her spear the bread with the fork and he held her arm, protectively, as she held it over the red coals. Dee soon realised that her supporting tactics were paying off dividends. Guy was beginning to show signs that he was actually enjoying her company – and that was good. Very good!

She munched the toast and sipped the tea, which was a little strong, graciously offering him further rein to foist his enthusiasm upon her. What had she to lose? Here she was breakfasting with him, wearing his pyjamas and jacket, and sharing his private, if not primitive way of life. Apart from attaining the status of his acceptance, she was slowly learning to accept the wisdom of his ways.

On any normal morning, she would have been stuck in front of her hotel dressing-table – cleaning, toning and emulsifying and carrying out other major repair work to her aging complexion – and spending an interminable amount of time deciding what to wear before going down to give her usual head-turning approach to the silver-plate and pure-white linen of the breakfast table. Instead of all that, here she was ludicrously half-submerged in masculinity – a hacking jacket and a pair of creased pyjamas and not a trace of make-up nor a golden hair in place. Heaven knows what she looked like, but it didn't seem to matter. It certainly didn't seem to matter to Mr. Anderson, who was happily rambling on about someone called old George who had ten cats and lived down the lane.

Listening wasn't one of her best assets, but it came a hell of a lot easier when Guy Anderson was doing the talking. *Very strange how absorbed he seems to be with this place*, she thought, *it's all so out of character with his professional image*. It was a side of him that she had never seen before and it was giving her a slightly uncomfortable feeling of insecurity. She was there with him and after last night in that grotty little bedroom, she'd never been closer and yet, it seemed that she was still on the outside looking in.

As Guy talked on, engrossed in his account of this old character's lethal parsnip wine, Dee was watching the sensitive curves of his mouth and thrilling to the recollection of the aftermath of his horrific nightmare when she'd cradled him in her arms. As his voice droned pleasantly on, she was secretly reliving the moments of his savage response to the lure of her vulnerable warmth. The ruthless, unrestrained subjection she'd undergone when supporting his full bodyweight; the droned ardent words of passion such as she'd never dared to hope for and that unexpected, sustained virility and power, which had consumed every part of her. So much for the callous words of that shallow ex-wife of his!

Only one thing had disturbed her, and was visibly disturbing her now as she remembered that exquisite moment of mutual orgasm when he'd croaked out a name that wasn't hers. Mary. Twice he'd said it – and then again, more gently, as he'd drifted off into the sleep that followed. *Who the hell is Mary?* She'd drifted off into her own sublime sleep, accepting the fact that it was no more than a blasphemous utterance on reaching his climax. Now, in the light of day, she was not so sure. On contemplation, Guy would never have used such an utterance. She tried to put the doubt out of her mind, but it became such an obsessive taunt that enquiry became a necessity. She reached for a cigarette, placing it in her mouth and lighting-up before drawing a long inward breath to quell her nerves.

"Who is Mary?" she asked lightly.

55

Through the cloud of smoke drifting into his direction, she saw that his expression had changed quite dramatically, and there was a stunned silence before he spoke.

"Who told you about Mary?"

"You did."

"Come off it, Dee! 'Bron must have told you!"

"Oberon? What's he got to do with it?"

"He's the only person I told!" Guy raised his voice in frustration.

"Then, I'd like to share the privilege…"

"How much did he tell you, Dee?"

"Tell me? I've told you, Oberon hasn't told me anything! I've not spoken to the man for days!"

"Then, who told you about Mary?"

"You did – last night! Don't tell me you've forgotten saying it."

"I don't remember saying anything to you. What did I say, exactly?"

"You said MARY! And stop pretending, Guy. You said it at least three times!"

He stared at her for a moment before turning his gaze into the fire. "Yes, now I remember saying it. It was when I was dreaming, wasn't it?"

"No! Not in the dream! It was after that – when we were making love!"

"Making love?" He gave her an incredulous look.

"Would you rather call it shagging?" she said, losing her patience with him. "Frankly, I hate the word!"

"Me too, but what do you mean when you say we made love last night? Surely you mean yesterday morning?"

Now, Dee was absolutely livid. "I may be bloody menopausal, but I'm not losing my mind! I've got the bruises to prove it!

"Bruises?"

"I'm not complaining about the bruises, Guy! I'd go to hell and back for what we had going for us last night!"

He was staring at her almost suspiciously.

"For heaven's sake, Guy – have I hit a raw nerve or something?" She stubbed out the cigarette before erupting into fury. "You're surely not trying to deny that last night we made love upstairs in that grotty little room? If we didn't, then some other lusty sod must had popped into the bed with me, whilst you were having it off with someone called Mary!"

"It's all a dream! You don't understand!" Guy protested.

"You're damned right, I don't!" She rose sharply to her feet and glared down at him. "Dreams? Let me assure you, lover – I've been off to dreamland and fantasy-land with you many times in the past, but this is the first time I've ever come back with love bites to prove it!" She tearfully snatched at the buttons on the pyjama-top to reveal the patchy purple marks displayed on her upper-half. "And Guy, if this acute loss of memory is your way of deviating from Mary whoever-she-is, then you're a bigger shit than I thought you were! Her voice broke into a sob a she forcefully stubbed out her cigarette and made for the door. Guy grabbed at her arm and forced her back with great precision to her seat by the fire.

"Listen, Dee, calm down, please, and let me explain. I'm beginning to realise what must have happened last night. Believe me, it isn't that I've forgotten the love-making at all."

"Oh, that's big of you!"

With great tenderness, his fingers traced the marks on her breasts before doing up the buttons on the pyjama-top. "Yes, I remember almost everything, but…"

"But what?" she snapped.

"I remember it as a dream. A truly wonderful dream. We were trying for a baby!"

"Oh, please!"

"Not you and me, Dee; Mary and me! I was still in the dream. I remember it so clearly, Dee! I was making love to her – promising to give her a child before I went away. I didn't know I was making love to you at the same time, I swear it! That wasn't me! It was her husband – Edward! Don't you see – it was him making love to you!"

Dee's cool gaze was rigid with contempt – and accompanied by a markedly slow hand-clap.

"Bravo! Who wrote the script?" The full force of her venom was upon him. "What a bloody fool I've been! I was ready to eat dirt for you – but I won't go lower than you! I know a shit when I see one!"

"Listen, Dee, please listen…"

"No, you listen! I'm getting out of this crummy little hovel and going back to civilisation. You're welcome to this lot and you're welcome to that slut; Mary! I hope her husband finds out and gives you just what you deserve, you bastard!" She hurled his jacket from her shoulders, throwing it onto the floor in a tearful rage.

"But Dee, you're jumping to all the wrong conclusions! You're being ridiculous, as usual!"

"Yes, I am ridiculous! A poor, pathetic, ridiculous woman for being here in the first place. Well, never again! Here, take your blasted pyjamas, they make me feel dirty!" She tore off the top and kicked off the bottoms, displaying her complete nudity before screaming at him with mounting hysteria. "Go on – take a long, hard look at an old has-been! Just useful enough to fantasize about Mary with!"

"Dee, you're beautiful – and you don't understand any of this. There's so much I've got to explain to you, my darling..."

"Explain it to Mary!" She stumbled to the door in a rage of tears.

"MARY DOES NOT EXIST!" Guy exclaimed, angrily.

At that moment, the framed text on the wall fell from its hook with such force that it showered the quarried floor with fragments of glass. The two of them turned to stare at it; and Guy was still staring at it as Dee ran naked from the room.

56

Guy watched Dee's black-topped Mini as it shot off down the lane. To the very last second, she'd dramatically waived his every effort to prevent her leaving. As she'd hastily gathered her bits and pieces together, she'd indulged herself in the sheer ruthless enjoyment of having him hovering over her in vain. Beseeching with her in the bedroom, then following her protesting down the stairway to open the door where, with great drama and an air of triumph, she'd made her way into the lane. After his fruitless attempts to stop her getting into the car, she'd finally strapped herself in, turned the key and zoomed away like a rocket from its launch-pad.

Guy waited until the hell-for-leather sounds of her departing acceleration were whizzed away into silence. As he then slowly mounted the five stone steps, he could only pray that she wasn't going to meet any unsuspecting traffic on those narrow bends. He winced at the thought of her coming into contact with the tractor or milk-truck.

Before going back inside the cottage, he lingered in the outer porch-way, thoughtfully running a forefinger over the peeling paintwork above the lintel. This time it seemed he'd completely blown it with Dee for good. He would normally have been relieved about that, but now he was feeling very dejected about the whole incident. He realised how insensitive he'd been to bring her here in the first place – but then, on reflection, she hadn't given him much alternative. *Come off it, you bastard*, he inwardly admitted, *you had every alternative; you only had to book another taxi!* For one reason or another, he knew he must have wanted her to come back with him. With this admonishment, he strode into the doorway, directing himself towards the telephone in the sitting-room.

"Hello? 'Bron? Oh, thank the Lord it's you! *'Fraid* we've got a problem again. I hate to say it, but we have!" There was an immediate groan on the other end of the line.

"Don't tell me! I'd been half-expecting it when I realised Lady Davidson didn't come down to breakfast this morning. Oh dear – and I was beginning to hope that you two were getting it nice and cosily together, dear."

"We were. That is until we had an unfortunate little bust-up – well, I suppose I would call it a big bust-up! Anyway, she's on her way back to the hotel."

"I don't like the sound of that, Guy love."

"It's not too serious, 'Bron. I was just ringing to say that she may start quizzing you about something, and I was hoping you could smooth the way."

"Smooth the way? When Delia's got one on her, she's like a time bomb in motion – and I don't intend to stand around waiting for her to explode, thank-you-very-much, dear!"

"Tell me about it!" Guy said, despondently.

"Honestly, you do put me through it, don't you, Guy love?"

"Yes, I do. Sorry about that, but if it's any comfort to you, it's me she's walked out on, not the play."

"I fear, then, that she might have walked out on the play as well! Can you tell me what happened? If I'm going to bear the brunt of it all, I'd like to be prepared. I don't wish to pry into your private affairs, but have you been a brute again, dear?"

"That's precisely why I'm ringing, 'Bron. I've not been a brute as you put it. I've been misunderstood, and I'm hoping you'll be able to calm her down before tonight's performance."

"Sorry, Guy. As much as I love you, I'm not in the mood for facing the wrath of an irate prima-donna this morning..."

"You'd rather have her walking-out, would you?"

"But you said..."

"I know what I said. Up to now, she's only walked out on me, and frankly, 'Bron, it's up to you to see that she doesn't walk out on the play!"

"Well, if that doesn't just take the biscuit! I'm absolutely speechless!"

"You're not going to have to make a speech, 'Bron. You're merely going to have to provide a few answers."

"What kind of answers?"

"When Dee gets back to the hotel and starts quizzing you, she's going to ask you about Mary. All I want you to do is tell her everything I told you."

"Everything?" Oberon asked, vaguely.

"Everything I told you about Mary, okay?"

"Mary who, for heaven's sake?"

"Surely you remember me telling you about Mary?"

"Quite contrary. No, you've lost me, Guy love."

"Come on, man! Cast your mind back to yesterday morning over coffee. The talk we had about Mary Ann Barker?"

"Oh no, dear. Not *that* Mary!" There was a long moan. "There's no wonder Delia's on her way back here if you've been trying to spin her that ghostly yarn! I thought you'd sorted all that out yesterday when you went to her room?"

"I'm afraid I spun her another yarn yesterday, simply because I knew she wouldn't swallow the truth!"

"And you think she'll swallow the truth from me?" Dream on, dear!"

"I did dream, 'Bron – and apparently, I rambled on in my sleep about Mary, calling her out by name, and of course, Dee heard me! I do remember calling out her name. God knows what else I said, but it was some dream, 'Bron."

"I see – and Delia being Delia, thinks that this Mary you were rambling on about was a flesh-and-blood rival?"

"Right!"

"Well, are you surprised, dear?"

"Look, my old friend, I'm not prepared to go into details at this moment, but let me assure you that there is more to this than anyone would realise – fact really is stranger than fiction, and I want you to make sure that Dee understands that. Simply confirm that I had already spoken to you about Mary being a ghost at this cottage and try to convince her, for all our sakes, that Mary no longer..." He paused, casting a furtive glance around the room. "...that Mary no longer exists!"

"Mary no longer exists" Oberon repeated wryly. "You must be off your trolley if you think she's going to accept that explanation from me. I value my frail personage too much to stand and take the consequences, however, I'm prepared to put my head on the block and take a chance."

"Thank you, that's a relief!"

"Now listen, Guy love, listen to the wisdom of an old fool; but one who has your best interests at heart. I'm beginning to get alarm signals from you – and that's putting it mildly. Even Ronnie's noticed the change in you and he's not the only one! Take last night, for example – you were as white as death and pissed out-of-your-mind! I really don't know how you managed to get through the performance – and now, dear, all this inane drivel about female spectres and people not existing; it really is enough to give you nightmares! I have to say it, Guy, if you're not careful, all this could have a devastating effect on your image with the public. Dabbling around in the paranormal is an extremely dangerous thing to do! After hearing you on the chat-show the other night, we were all so proud of you; it was real fighting talk and it silenced those tabloids for good! You've got everything going for you again and you don't have to go off in search of the supernatural for kicks – so take my advice, Guy love, and get out of that spooky cottage, now, before you become completely obsessed. In my opinion, you're half-obsessed already! We've got four more nights to run here in the Potteries and then we're off to the West-end! You've got to be in good shape for that – we all have!"

"Have you finished?"

"We love you, Guy, and we're all concerned!"

"I don't need your concern, 'Bron. I'm not going through my mid-life crisis either. I've been through all that with Roxanne – and I'm certainly not dabbling in the paranormal! This cottage isn't spooky – not in the sense that you mean; it's very primitive and basic as Dee will probably tell you, but to me it has charisma and charm – and for me, though I can't explain it, there's something meaningful about being here. I'm not obsessed; moreover intrigued, and I have no intention of becoming obsessed. Does that put your mind at rest?

"I still think you'd be better away from April Cottage, Guy."

"I will be on Saturday, but not a day before!"

"Please yourself!" Oberon said, suitably defeated.

"Now..." Guy continued. "If Dee makes any silly threats about walking-out on the play again, ring me, and I'll be straight over to sort her out, but if you tell her what I told you, there shouldn't be a problem – and tell her that I've been doing some considerable research and I've uncovered some tangible facts; for instance, Mary Ann Barker lived here in the early nineteen-forties – and she died here in childbirth – and therefore; Mary Ann Barker does not exist anymore – only in the spirit world! As I told you before, 'Bron, I've discovered her grave in the local church-yard. It was hidden beneath piles of thorns; remind Dee how I still have the scratch marks to prove I'd been there – and tell her that it's common knowledge amongst the locals that her spirit remains in the cottage! She's waiting for the husband who never came back, because he was shot down over Germany during the war! Tell her that's what my nightmare was all about – and hopefully, it might just convince her that I'm telling the truth!"

There was a long sigh from the production manager as he'd wearily been trying to come to terms with what he was hearing. "I wish you'd booked in here at the hotel with the rest of us, Guy. Whoever's responsible for allocating that venue to you is going to get more than a piece of my mind! I intend to tackle administration about it; it's a disgrace to think that you, Guy Anderson, should be given a place reputed to be haunted, not to mention the fact that it's way below the standards to which you are accustomed!"

"Forget it, 'Bron. One way or another, I would have turned up here at April Cottage. I was destined to come. I know it. I can feel it. I have a kind of bizarre fascination for the place and I intend to find out why. So, try to explain that to Dee. Tell her that I love her and that I'll talk to her tonight, after the show."

"Very well" Oberon conceded. Before he could utter another word, Guy had hung-up the phone.

57

The framed text was back in its place above the mantelpiece, minus the splinters of glass, which Guy has diligently and carefully removed from every crevice in the quarried tiles. With the murkiness of its glass covering gone, the former pristine condition of the ornate, black lettering and its colourful embellishment of white lilies was pleasantly revealed. Now, it was an object to be admired and revered - he had a strange kind of empathy with that particular item. He felt responsible for the breakage and decided that he should have it re-glazed. Again, he reached up to remove it from the wall. As he inched the thick cord over the rusty hook, he began to question how on earth it had fallen in the first place. The cord was intact and the hook was firmly in position. He couldn't abandon the thought that it had dropped with such velocity at the precise moment when he'd made the declaration that Mary Ann Barker didn't exist.

Mary did exist! She was making it expressively clear to him that she existed. His trembling fingers placed the framework of lettering and lilies down onto the table. *She exists alright! She's here now! In this room!* Guy was hair-raisingly aware of her extreme closeness to him. He knew that he only had to raise his eyes in the direction of the doorway to the scullery where the waft of perfume was emanating its strange allurement.

PREPARE TO MEET THY GOD.

He gained little or no comfort from those ominous words staring up at him from the table top. Instead, there was but one ice-cold compulsion – to turn his petrified gaze and see the ghostly form of Mary Ann Barker, standing behind him.

58

The screaming silence was riveted with the ripples of Mary's resounding voice calling melodiously around the room.

"Edward? E d w a r d?"

It was such a girlish voice and it rang with the restlessness of youth; a voice he knew – or had known, and when at last his eyes were relentlessly drawn towards her face it was a face he knew – or had known!

"M a r y!" He breathed out the word unrestrainedly as he stared into the aura of deep violet light. The vibrant forces of belonging and recognition surged like a belt of magnetism between them. Her face was radiant with a knowing smile, which seemed to be saying that Edward was home again. In that swift, enhanced moment, his whole being was possessed and uplifted towards the unification of their yearning souls.

The encounter was briefer than brief! The light of her countenance departed in a meteoric second and Guy was left to stare through the void of the curtained doorway and beyond; and left to question the sheer improbability of whether it had happened or not. Moments ago, he'd been mystically hovering over his own body – levitating in time and space. Now, for the first time, with the coldness of the quarried floor beneath his trembling feet, he was scared!

59

Thank God for the fresh morning air and grass beneath your feet. Guy had fled from the room and found the sanctity of the garden. He wandered, vague and disorientated, along the narrow pathway, snatching his fingers at the tops of various plants and bushes. Reaching the small wooden gate, he leaned against it; finding stability in the sturdiness of the weatherworn wood. It was some time before his quivering limbs and all the palpitations going on inside him had subsided; and some time before he could turn to take a long and troubled backward look at the cottage with its fringe of ivy and yellowing brickwork.

Beyond the wooden portal arrangement, the door was still open as he'd left it; relentlessly beckoning his return.

60

"Your afternoon tea, sir."

"Put it down, thanks" Guy said absently, without turning his gaze from the Minton room's great bay-window. Below him across the street was the deserted frontage of the railway station. He watched vacantly as a rolled-over litter bin rocked like a cradle in the breeze, strewing its contents over the cobblestones.

"Oh, sorry, hang on a moment..." Guy turned to offer a tip. The youthful attendant acknowledged it gratefully and left in dutiful silence as the massive door swung to a close, making a decisive locking sound.

Guy glanced down at the tray, which was elegantly cluttered with plated tea-ware and an assortment of fancy cakes. Pulling up a chair, he sat down and idly tinkered about with the cup, saucer and spoon whilst moodily contemplating the circumstances that had once again resulted in yet another slice of hotel life.

His departure from April Cottage had been remorseless and swift. Two large bags, hastily bunged up with his belongings, stood unopened on the suitcase stand and they would now remain there until he left for London at the end of the week. Using hotel wardrobes and drawers gave him a feeling of permanence to which he objected; he preferred to rummage through his bags for whatever he needed.

As much as he objected to this sudden change of environment, Guy was conscious of having made the right decision. Nobody in their right mind would have stayed on at the cottage to experience further freakish abnormalities. Here, within the very safe solidarity of this buff-coloured, four-walled mausoleum, with the sound of trains and traffic going by, his memory was thankfully clouded with all the uncertainty of what had happened. Mary's ghost seemed so ludicrously unreal now, and he began to assume that he must have been suffering from severe hallucinations.

The tea was comfortingly hot and a couple of sugary-looking cakes went down easily. He hadn't eaten since breakfast; such had been his haste to vacate the cottage. None of the cast had been around when he stepped into the foyer. The younger ones would probably be happily rambling, incognito, around the Five-Towns. Oberon and Ronnie would no doubt be working on some project at the theatre, or failing that, Guy knew that 'Bron was hoping to visit the Potteries Museum and Art Gallery before the week was over – and, of course, old Henry would be slumped in his room until it was time for curtain-up – but, more importantly, where was Dee? Surely, she'd be in her room on the second floor, waiting to be consoled.

With the Wednesday-evening performance zooming ever closer, he reckoned that the best thing to do was to go along there to let her know he was now staying at the hotel. That alone would surely pacify her and from now on, he was going to make a conscious effort to improve their relationship. She was perhaps a little too possessive and volatile, but she was loyal – and she loved him! Maybe he was beginning to love her too. He'd been tempted to ring her room when he arrived but he'd decided against it. The two of them had some straight talking to do and it would have to be face-to-face.

61

Guy had been knocking upon Dee's hotel-room door for some time. She wasn't there. He paced up and down the corridor, deciding upon his next move. Checking his watch, he realised there was only three and a half hours to go, and before then there was undoubtedly some patching up to be done.

He shot back to his own room to ring the theatre, only to find that none of the cast were available - it seemed they were all out. He moved to the window, looking down over the fleet of cars on the forecourt. The black-topped Mini wasn't there. Guy rang reception.

"Room number please?"

"The Minton Room!" Guy snapped, impatiently.

"Oh, sorry – Mr. Anderson, sir. How can I help?"

"I've been trying to contact Miss Delia Davidson. I've called her room, but there's no answer. Can you tell me if she's out, please?"

"Miss Davidson checked-out this morning, sir."

"Right, thanks." Guy replaced the receiver and stared unbelievingly into space. Dee had left the hotel. *What a crazy, senseless and utterly childish thing to do! This is real trouble!*

Within minutes, he was on his way to the theatre where, he suspected, panic stations would be in operation. Oberon would certainly have been trying to contact him at the cottage to say that Delia had checked-out. He passed the Potteries Museum and Art Gallery as he approached the city-centre and, under the circumstances, discounted the possibility of Oberon being there. He would be far too busy to follow his usual delight of looking at prehistoric artefacts when there was a leading-lady missing.

When he walked through the stage-door, there wasn't a soul about and his footsteps echoed intrusively as he wandered in and out of the deserted dressing-rooms. He called out as he stepped onto the open stage and his voice resounded up and beyond the flies and out across the darkened auditorium with its rows and rows of empty seats.

Completely mystified by the absence of staff, he wended his way round to front-of-house and finally found larger-than-life Lorna. She was perched like a puffin on a nest, filling every ounce of space within the glass confines of the box-office. She beamed at him like a full-moon through the aperture in the glass.

"Mr. Anderson! My hero in person! I'm glad you've finally turned up!"

"Where is everyone, Lorna?"

"I don't know, but everyone has been after you! Mr. Mercer has been doing his nut! I don't know whether you know, but Miss Davidson's walked-out! It's been like bedlam here all day!"

"Well, it's quietened down a bit now – there's no-one backstage – it's like a morgue in there! Do you know where Mr. Mercer is now?"

"Not-a-clue, duck, but I know he's in a bit of a flap. Everyone is!"

The telephone rang and she picked up the receiver, cupping her hand over the mouth-piece to confide in him. "I only hope this doesn't mean we have to cancel! I know they're doing their best to get an understudy, but from what I can gather they're not having much joy!" She turned her attention to the phone. "Hello, Theatre Royal. Can I help? Oh, sorry madam, there are no tickets left for this evening's performance! Absolutely certain, madam. So, sorry. Goodbye."

62

Guy moved along the carpeted corridor to the theatre manager's office but found it closed. He returned to back-stage and decided to wait in the green-room until someone showed up. Sitting there in that dreary, little room, staring at the shoddiness of the raspberry coloured walls, he began to despair of the situation. How could the play go on without Dee? Her understudy had left weeks ago, and if Oberon was trying to contact her, he'd be finding it difficult to say the least. Bella Townsend was renowned for being a disagreeable character who enjoyed the drama of being so.

He began remonstrating with himself again. He was the one to blame in all of this. He should have known how Dee would have reacted under such circumstances. He should have persuaded her to stay much more firmly than he did. They should have sat down and talked it through. *Then again, it's easy to be wise after the event.*

Upon hearing voices, he rose and went to the door. Ronnie was coming down the passage and when he saw Guy, he turned and ran back to call Oberon, who was outside the stage-door, having some kind of hot flush. The two of them then came cavorting along towards him with 'Bron feverishly mopping his brow with a flowered handkerchief.

"Guy love! We've been ringing you like fury! If I'd remembered the directions to your cottage, I'd have driven over to see you, dear! We're all having such a terrible time. Where were you when we needed you?"

"At the Five Towns Hotel! I took your advice and left the cottage. I checked-in at the hotel to find that Dee has checked-out. Since then, I've been looking for you!"

"Well we must have been on opposite sides of the planet! Haven't you seen her again? I was hoping she'd have contacted you by now?"

"I've not seen or heard anything from her. What is the woman playing at?"

"Search me, dear! After you called this morning, I chased all over the place trying to contact her, only to find she'd checked-out of the hotel."

"You mean you let her go without telling her any of the stuff I told you to tell her?" Guy boomed, walking off in the direction of the stage. "For God's sake, man, I took the trouble of ringing you this morning! All this could have been avoided if you'd just done what I asked!" He strode out beneath the proscenium arch and his wrath went out into the vast hollowness of the auditorium, "I told you that it was up to you to stop her walking-out on the play! I rang in plenty of time for you to catch her arriving back at the hotel! Well, didn't I? Instead of giving me your motherly advice, you should have been straight up to the second-floor to stop her leaving! Now, thanks to you, we're minus our female lead – and that means no show!"

Oberon Mercer, now all flair, flounce and majesty followed him to centre-stage with a voice projection that would have done justice to Hamlet. "Come, come Sir Guy – time to climb down from your extra-high horse! Nothing to be gained by casting blame on an innocent bystander! Let me assure you – yours truly is completely innocent – and may I say, completely devastated! This is *my* production! Without Vanda Fairchild, we're sunk! As far as I'm concerned, there is only one person to play Vanda and that is Miss Delia Davidson, and who is responsible for her absence? Certainly not Oberon J. Mercer!" His pomp and ceremony continued. "I waited for her to appear in the hotel foyer this morning, just as you'd suggested. When she didn't come, I took the trouble to go to her room. She wasn't there, so I asked at reception about her, only to be told that she'd checked-out without a word to anyone. Except to Ronnie! He just happened to be on the car park when she went to her car. 'Give Guy Anderson a message for me' she said, 'tell him to find a new leading-lady and tell him to…' - well, I believe the expletive to be quite a strong one for a lady. Isn't that right, Ronnie, love?" Ronnie mumbled in support and disappeared into the wings.

"I'm sorry, my old friend. Very sorry indeed." Guy flopped onto the set's floral settee, thumping at the cushions in disgust with himself. "As you say, 'Bron, I'm entirely to blame for this whole miserable situation, and I apologise to everyone concerned, especially you. I very much regret the way I spoke to you just now. Please forgive me."

Oberon went to immediately comfort and commiserate with Guy and the two of them sat side-by-side at centre-stage, staring out at the rows and rows of empty seats, which would soon be filling for tonight's fully-booked performance.

"They tell me there's a civic party coming in tonight with a drinks party to follow in the bar. The Lord-Mayor of Stoke-on-Trent and other dignitaries will be here, not to mention the local press. We've got to do something, Guy love."

"I know. I'm racking my brains trying to think of where Dee could have gone. She doesn't know this area at all. If only I'd…" Guy put his head in his hands as Oberon laid a comforting hand on his shoulder. "I suppose you've tried Bella Townsend, 'Bron?"

"Yes. She's on another production so there's no hope there! I've tried everyone including Violet, who might have known someone, but she was unavailable. I've an idea she's touring Europe with another company."

"What about the A.S.M.?" Guy suggested. "She's done us some big parts."

"My assistant stage manager could only do it with a script. I'd rather cancel!"

"We can't cancel, 'Bron! We can't! I've got to find Dee. I'll get on to her agent."

"Done that! He's heard nothing and he hasn't got a clue to where she might be. We can only sit it out and hope to hear from him."

"Sit it out? It's almost five-o-clock! We can't sit around waiting!"

"There's not a lot you can do, dear – unless you know someone who could play Vanda Fairchild. How about Roxanne?"

"How about a clip round the ear?"

"Sorry, love – I'm just jesting with you."

The two of them turned as a cacophony of approaching voices was heard in the wings. The young trio: Kat, Max and Rodney made their anxious entrance onto the stage.

"Is it true? Has the silly cow finally walked-out on us?" Kat asked.

"Yes!" Oberon replied in a tired voice.

"Oh, fuck!" Rodney played up to the gallery.

"The bitch! Let *me* do it?" Kat insisted.

"And who'd do yours, sweetie?" Oberon asked, flicking his floral handkerchief in her direction. "Anyway, you're too young!"

"Well, it looks like we're in the shit then!" Max said with disgust.

"You could say that, love." Oberon replied, regrettably.

"You mean we might have to ditch the show?" Kat's eyes were on pivots as she waited for a reply, but there was none forthcoming.

Guy rose from the settee and walked away from the small company. He moved slowly upstage through the French-windows to the artificiality of the patio with its boxed hydrangeas; the spot where old Henry's Ezra Jackson met his death each evening. *Not much chance of that taking place tonight*, Guy thought, ruefully. He sat in Ezra's cane chair and looked out despairingly at the small group, huddled together at centre-stage.

A chilling silence fell over the entire building as the minutes progressed towards the deadline hour of six-o-clock, when the decision to cancel the evening's performance would have to be made. The two local radio stations had already been briefed about the possibility of the play being cancelled, and both were awaiting a decision before making any informative broadcasting on the subject.

Just before six, Henry arrived at the stage-door. No-one had bothered to tell him anything and he must have wondered what on earth was going on when he found the players and staff mooching despondently around on stage.

"Hello there, Henry!" Guy called to him, rising from the cane chair. "Not too comfortable, this chair of yours!"

"Damned uncomfortable! Now you know why I complain. Done irreparable damage to my posterior!"

"Well it doesn't look as though you'll be required to sit on it tonight, old boy!"

"Why? Have they given me another? About time!"

"They haven't told you then, Henry?"

"Told me what?"

Guy continued to explain all the details of Dee's disappearing act to Henry. The older man gave a merry little chuckle.

"I wondered what all the long faces were for!" He lit his cigar and laughed again. "Well, well, well. So, the delightful Duchess has finally pulled out all the stops. I must say, Guy, I've seen this coming for weeks!"

"Well I wish you'd have warned me about it!"

"You wouldn't have heeded it if I had! You'd have told me to sober up – but, you know what they say – nothing like a drunken man for the truth! Well, well, well – Good for the Duchess, I say."

"What? You silly old fool! She's walked-out and stopped the show!"

"Always told her she was a show-stopper!" He pushed out his ample belly and grinned. "She can bring my curtain down any night. Lovely looking woman is the Duchess."

"Is that all you have to say about it?"

"What else is there to say?"

"There's a hell of a lot I'd like to say, but it isn't going to bring her back if I do. She's walked-out on us and there's nothing we can do about it!"

"Walked-out on you, Guy! Not us. It's you she's trying to impress. Don't you see? It's the only way she can get through to you. Some fellows get all the luck."

"Luck? Am I hearing you correctly? Am I supposed to be pleased that she's walked-out on me and ruined the performance for everyone else? It's going to cost thousands! Look at poor old 'Bron – he's devoted to this play and its cast! And look at those three young ones – this is their first big-break in the theatre, do they look pleased?

Hundreds of people are going to be turned away at the door tonight – even the Lord Mayor and Co. – and why? Because of that silly little bitch who never had a single thought in her head for anyone but herself!" Guy had raised his voice to such a degree that everyone had turned to stare at him and were now hanging on his every word. "What does she care about all these people who are standing around here and wondering if they're going to work tonight? What does she care about all the folk who've paid bloody good money for their seats? Does she give a DAMN about any of us?"

"Yes. I do" called a beautifully controlled voice. "And that's precisely why I'm here."

Every head in the place turned to see the lone figure, walking elegantly down the centre-aisle of the stalls towards the stage. There was a chorus of gleeful accord, which resounded throughout the building. The cast quickly dissipated, turning quietly and respectfully to go about their business in preparation for the show, leaving a man and *his* leading-lady, gazing at each other across the footlights.

63

There was an air of celebration that evening following the performance. Cast and crew had gathered in the green-room to complement each other whilst several other notables had gate-crashed to give their idolatry congratulations. It had been a special evening, mainly due to the mayoral party who had visited back-stage after the show, adding their prestigious presence to the occasion.

Guy was taking a back seat for a change, happily allowing his leading-lady to claim the limelight – and deservedly so. He was sitting in the corner with old Henry, who was putting away his usual pint.

"After all that Much-ado, she gave the performance of her life!" Henry beamed.

"Wonderful!" Guy replied, admiringly.

"High time the Duchess had a bit of recognition. She puts her heart, body and soul into it, you know!?"

"Oh, I know it, Henry – boy, do I know it!"

The two of them watched Dee gesticulating with a group of admirers; flaunting herself and revelling within the aura of their gratification. Tonight, she was the heroine who saved the show; she was the prodigal daughter! Tonight, she'd gone on the stage to give Vanda such eloquence, such style and realism.

Consequently, Guy's Trevor Adams had responded inspirationally and the rapport between the two players was better, classier and more meaningful than ever before. Their final kiss had neem so utterly consuming that it kept the packed audience waiting, engaged in emotion. Until the great Theatre Royal curtain had fallen. The applause had then been tumultuous and easily the best the tour had received to date. Henry and Guy agreed that these Pottery folks had certainly enjoyed the riveting new play and knew how to show their appreciation.

The euphoria of it all gradually began to die away as tired, but happy people made their eventual departure from the green-room. Guy needed to go along to his dressing-room to pick up his things – and he motioned for Dee to follow him. As they prepared to leave, old Henry shot them a wink, chuckling into his beer.

64

"Close the door" Guy ordered as soon as they'd reached his dressing-room. Dee obeyed and turned to face him. Her face was lit with triumph. "You were truly wonderful tonight, darling. I don't have to tell you that because you know you were!" Guy meant every word.

"You were wonderful too, but then, you always are!" They stood looking at each other without moving.

"Come here" he said, quietly.

She walked into his open arms and he held her so lovingly and so silently until everything else in the world ceased to be. She leaned against his shoulder, feeling safe and more secure than she'd felt in years.

"Let's go back and talk. Just talk" Guy said meaningfully.

"Yes, that is if you'll come back to the hotel first. I can't face going back to that cottage, sorry."

"You don't have to, and neither do I! As you checked-out of the hotel this morning, my lovely, I checked-in."

"You mean...?" her voice sprang into the treble clef. "You mean you'll be staying at the hotel tonight?"

"Yes – and for the rest of the week! So, let's get back there now and have some supper in my room and talk – and Dee, I did say *talk!*"

"Whatever gave you the idea that I would want to do anything else?" She gave him a provocative look and then waited while he gathered his belongings together. When, moments later, they stepped out of the stage-door as a twosome, into the night, her delight knew no bounds.

65

Delia Davidson gave the Minton-room the kind of lovely ornamentation it could only have known in the past, that would be somewhere between the trendy-twenties and the theatrical-thirties. Guy watched her with amusement as she went swanning off into the bathroom in a crimson, silk dressing-gown. Heads must have surely turned as the shoulder-padded vision of elegance floated down the stairway and along to his room on the first floor; though, he assumed, at that hour, most heads would have been on pillows.

Only crumbs were left on the plates where the beef and horseradish sandwiches had been and the coffee-pot was empty. The two of them had enjoyed the room-service supper, discussing the improved performance in their individual roles; analysing and planning on how they would inject that inspired whatever-it-was into the forthcoming West-end premiere.

Guy poured himself a tall glass of Beaujolais and pronounced that it was time to talk about other matters. More personal matters. Dee had readily agreed, saying that he still had a lot of explaining to do, and then excused herself to pay a quick visit to the rest-room. In her brief absence, Guy was left to consider what was to be gained by confronting Dee with a lot of unnecessary details concerning him and why he'd left April Cottage. Could he expect someone like her to understand the strange phenomena, which continued to haunt him even now, when it was all resolutely behind him; locked away there? Could he ever make her believe in the transitory existence of Mary Ann Barker in the way that he had come to believe? It was likely that such revelations could blow their relationship sky-high, but if the relationship was going to have any lasting qualities, Dee had got to know about the startling events of the last few days. He needed her to know. He wanted her to know.

"Positively archaic, that bathroom!" Dee exclaimed, emerging in a cloud of menthol smoke. "Now then, I believe you have something to say, and I'm all ears." She moved the small armchair near to him. "Well, Guy darling, speak to me."

"Do you have to smoke those things?" he said, wafting the smoke away.

"Sorry, I wasn't aware of the no-smoking sign!" Immediately on the offensive, she stubbed it out.

Not the best of starts, Guy thought, annoyed with himself for saying anything. "Here, let me light you another one. I really don't mind if you smoke." He held out the open packet and after much deliberation, she took one and he lit it for her.

"Thank you" Dee said, settling down again into the armchair. "I know I'm seen as a positive health-hazard, but if you want me to stay awake whilst we talk, I shall have to insist on having a cigarette in my hand."

"I know – and I hope I didn't sound too pernickety. I'm getting tired too, shall we leave it until morning?"

"It's morning now, Guy, and you're not going to get out of it that easily! You've promised to enlighten me about a certain lady called Mary. Well, go on – I can't wait to hear about her. I'm all agog!" She looked across at him with a kind of amused expectancy that had him hesitating even more.

"Okay. Do you remember, this morning at the cottage, when I asked you about reincarnation?"

"Yes..." She questioned him with an instant frown.

"I had a very strong reason for asking you that, Dee – and I still do! You see..." He hesitated again, wondering how he was going to make everything seem credible.

"Wait a minute, Guy – is that what this is all about? Reincarnation? I thought…"

"You thought what?"

"I thought, or rather hoped, that you were going to give me some sort of explanation for last night, not to mention this morning!"

"I am!"

"Well, what's all this reincarnation stuff got to do with it?"

"Everything!"

"Oh, come on, Guy! You disappoint me if you can't do better than that!" She impatiently crossed her legs and the crimson gown fell apart, revealing plenty of thigh. "I really don't want a load of excuses for your unreasonable behaviour. I want a truthful explanation. When you made love to me the way you did last night, for me it was Hosanna in the highest! That is until…well, let's face it, no woman wants to hear another woman's name whispered into her ear when she's just reached her glorious climax! Then, when you tried to fob me off this morning with some fabrication about it all being a dream…"

"That *was* the truth. You said you wanted a truthful explanation and that's what I'm giving you, Dee. I'll admit it here and now that I was totally unaware that I was making love to you last night. I was dreaming! Dreaming that I was Mary's husband, and that I was trying to…"

"Trying to get her bloody pregnant!" she pronounced, scornfully. "I think those were the words you used this morning before I walked out on you. If you're expecting me to swallow all that shit, I'm likely to walk out on you right now!"

His voice became imploring, "Please listen. I'm not trying to tell you a pack of lies in my defence. I really do need your understanding in all of this. I have to talk to someone about this, and God knows that I was hoping you'd be that someone. You see, I've become involved with something that is way beyond my understanding. That is the real reason why I packed up and left the cottage this morning. I'd reached the point where I was scared out of my wits."

66

Dee queried with a raised eyebrow as she stubbed out her cigarette. "Scared? You? You certainly never gave me the impression that you were scared. God knows why, but you seemed to be in your element with the place."

"I was…but when you'd left, that's when it happened!"

"When what happened?" She noticed that his expression had changed quite dramatically.

"I don't suppose that you're going to believe any of it."

"Try me" she said, adopting a more receptive attitude.

"Perhaps I should start at the beginning. When I first went to the cottage on Saturday morning, my immediate reaction was that I'd been there before. Everything about the place and its surroundings seemed very familiar to me, yet I knew that I had never set foot in the place before."

"Déjà vu?"

"Right – and I shook it off as being just that, after all, it's a common enough thing, apparently –

but then the weird things started to happen. On the very first night, I had this strangely realistic dream about a young woman who seemed to be registering from somewhere in my past. It was so real that I began to wonder if I'd actually been awake and seen it all taking place there in the bedroom! The next day, I began to sense unaccountable things; like the smell of drifting perfume and the swish of a skirt as if someone had passed me by. Then, on the second night – and this was awful, believe me – I heard the sounds of a woman, sobbing her heart out in the sitting-room; a woman obviously in great distress, but when I went in there, the room was empty and icy cold, yet I distinctly felt that there was someone in there; a kind of presence. It was uncanny. I think it was the following night – the night you rang me, when I told you someone was in the room with me..."

"The girl with the puncture?"

"I'm sorry. I had to concoct that story to pacify you. I knew you would never have believed me if I'd told you that I was looking at a ghost – but now, Dee, now you've simply got to believe me, because I'm telling you the truth. It was a ghost! The ghost of Mary Ann Barker, who'd once lived there at the cottage. I could describe her to you in detail; she was standing by the window, looking out. I didn't see her face, but I could visualise her features because I knew it was the girl I'd seen in the bedroom. As I watched her gazing out of the window, I knew that she was waiting for someone – someone who'd never returned. She'd been waiting for him for nearly fifty years."

"Supposing I believed you, how could you possibly know all that?" Dee asked, lighting another cigarette to counteract the creeping gooseflesh.

Guy proceeded to tell her everything that had led to his knowledge of Mary and her tragic past. How at first, he'd shrugged off the milkman's ludicrous description of a wailing ghost-woman until old George had filled him in with the facts that seemed to substantiate such a claim. Facts that told of Mary's unfortunate circumstances, back in the days of the war, when her husband had been killed in action; and facts revealing that she herself had died at April Cottage soon after, in childbirth.

"I had to find out if there was any truth in it all" Guy continued. "So, I went along to see if I could find Mary's grave in the little church-yard. Do you remember me pointing it out to you when we passed that row of houses?" Dee, now totally absorbed, nodded in silence. "Well, that's where I found her gravestone – hidden beneath masses of thorns. I could easily have overlooked it and walked away, but Dee, I *knew* it was there. Something or some*one* was telling me that it was there! So, I waded into the thorns and that's exactly how I came to have all these scratches on my arms."

"I presume you read the epitaph on the stone?"

"Yes. Just the name and date. I can see it now. Mary Ann Barker of April Cottage who departed this life in April nineteen forty-three." Guy drank the remainder of his wine and Dee fiddled with the gold ring on her left hand. "Then, last night that terrible nightmare of a dream was all about *his* death, but it was me who was experiencing every horrific moment."

"Whose death?"

"Edward Barker. The husband of Mary Ann Barker."

With Dee's attentiveness assured, Guy began to ramble on about the dream like someone possessed. "His plane was being hunted by the long pointing fingers of enemy searchlights; stalked like an intruder under Germany's night sky. Wing and fuselage were caught in a blinding shaft of light and exposed to a merciless bombardment of gunfire before eventually being brought down – but it was me who was piloting that plane when it came hurtling down in flames! It was me spiralling down and seeing that face in the clouds! Mary's face! It was all there in the dream, the agonising thought of leaving her alone forever;

and the despair of knowing that I would never see the face of our unborn child. The heat, the anguish, and that awful fear of dying! I remember the actual moment of impact! One usually wakes up from a dream at that dreadful type of climax, but no! When the plane hit the ground, I remember lying there, plunged into that dark abyss of blackness beyond; it was an inescapable vacuum – but then I was being drawn into the perspective of a distant white-light. I was being carried, cradled in someone's arms towards it. I remember thinking that this must be heaven! Mary and I were back together again, making love! Making such mystical love!" He sighed for a long moment.

"I know. I was there!" Dee said huskily, with tears welling in her eyes.

There was a haunted look in his eyes as he turned towards her. "Yes, and thank God you were there, Dee. I know now that it was your arms, carrying me and cradling me away from death and into the light. I know now that it was you and I making love. If you hadn't been there, Dee, I think I might have died in that room!"

APRIL COTTAGE

67

"What a pity you didn't listen to me when I told you to leave that cottage! Please, Guy, don't let all this get such a hold on you! To a point, I can understand that in your case, we all know how much you enjoy your solitude for a change; but why go to a place like that cottage. A cold, damp, dingy little hovel that's obviously had the most devastating effect on you, Guy. I can now see what's happened; you've been listening to the locals and their stupid tales, had a drink or two and it's all blown up into some kind of reality. Let's face it, Guy; it's easy enough for anyone to conjure up a vision of a lonely young widow, standing grieving by a window, waiting fifty years for her uniformed hero husband to return. If he'd been half as sexy and a quarter as handsome as you, I'd have stood there with her. Oh, come on, Guy, don't look at me like that! You've got to see the funny side of this!"

"Yes, I suppose it's funny to you." Guy rose rather sharply and went into the bathroom, closing and bolting the door behind him.

"Shit!" Dee cursed herself for bringing things to a halt with a highly insensitive remark. Her flippancy had been intended to console him rather than to infuriate him. She'd hoped that by making light of the situation, Guy would come to take things less seriously. *What a vain hope!* The truth was that he was quite seriously obsessed.

68

Everything pointed to the fact that he believed himself to be the living embodiment of Edward Barker who had been killed in the second-world-war. Dee was going over the things he'd told her; the feelings of déjà vu when he'd first arrived at the cottage; *and yes – when we talked on the phone, he'd spoken of perfume pervading the room – and there was that other phone-call when he talked of someone being in the room – and his account of the pilot's death had been incredibly realistic.* Dee herself had been witness to the fact that he'd cried out in his dream about the wing being on fire, followed by those tormented cries of 'Dear God, we're going down!'. That was when she'd held him and comforted him and soon after, they were headlong into the most wonderful session of love-making she'd ever experienced. That is until the name of Mary was called out with such feverish emotion.

Guy was normally the most level-headed of guys. Despite his fame as a stage idol, he was a totally unassuming person who was not given to histrionics or eccentric behaviour. *So why all of this? Why in the small hours would he want to embark on such a dramatic account?* He'd told her that he was genuinely scared. Was he really asking her to share his fears, and if so, shouldn't she be doing just that? She lit another cigarette and waited patiently for him to come out of the bathroom.

"Guy?" she said, rising towards him. "Why did you ask me if I believed in reincarnation?"

"Drop it now, Dee, let's get some shut-eye, shall we?" He brushed past her, removing his jacket.

"No, I want to know!" She followed him closely. "Why did you ask me about reincarnation?"

"I said forget it!" He threw his jacket onto the chair.

"Was it because you feel that you were once Mary's husband?" Guy swung round to face her. "I'm right, aren't I? You feel that you are the reincarnation of that man who died in the plane?"

To Guy, Dee's green eyes had never looked more receptive than they did at that moment. He could see that she was ready to believe in what he was trying to say. He took the cigarette from her and stubbed it into the ashtray, then leading her by the hand to the bed, he lifted her onto the top coverlet, resting her head on the pillow and gently smoothing down the crimson silk of her gown with his hands. Sitting on the bed beside her, he lowered his face towards her until their lips were touching.

"You're not just a tigress of a leading-lady with a pretty face, are you?" he said eventually, lifting his head to study her features. "I knew there was a warm understanding woman in there somewhere."

"It's very easy to be warm and understanding when you're in love with someone – and for the same reason, it's very easy to be silly and temperamental too. At this very moment, I could be anything you want me to be. It's my guess that at this moment in time, you need a good listener. Am I right?"

"You've listened enough for one evening. It can wait."

"No, it can't! I want to know everything, now! I want to share this with you, Guy! I want to know why you're so scared?"

"No, Dee" he immediately arose from the bed and stood with his back to her. "I want to forget it."

"But you won't forget it!" She lay there with perfect composure staring up at the glinting chandelier and determined to drag it out of him. "If you're not prepared to talk about it, Guy, it's going to eat you inside. Tell me why you were scared after I'd left this morning – so scared that you left the cottage to come here?"

"No!" he said, turning to face her again, then positioning himself on the edge of the bed. "I want you to forget it all now – all of it!"

"Don't be stupid! I can't forget it! Do you know why I can't forget it? Because I really believe now that you are scared – I can see it written all over your face. I can see it in your eyes and I'm very concerned for you. Don't tell me to forget it. Just tell me why – why you're afraid? Up until today, you've raved about that cottage so much that you've been prepared to put up with the fact that it is haunted! What happened this morning to change your mind? I know it wasn't because I left. I don't pride myself on that!"

After a thoughtful pause, he spoke to her softly but meaningfully. "I couldn't expect you or anyone else to believe what scared me."

"Just tell me!" she said, fiddling with his gold cuff-links.

"Soon after you'd gone this morning, I saw her again – for the first time she spoke to me." His voice diminished with each word.

"My God, that would scare anyone!"

"It scared the pants off me!"

"What did she say?" She held his hand firmly in hers. "Tell me."

"She was standing in the corner of the kitchen-room. I knew she was there before I saw her. I was afraid to turn and see her, but she compelled me to look."

"And...?"

"And I knew her. I really knew her - and she knew me. We just stood looking at each other like two people lost in time. Then she spoke, at least, I could hear her speaking but her lips never moved. She called me Edward – and just in that moment, I *was* Edward!"

"What happened then?"

"She simply disappeared, then I ran like a petrified rabbit into the garden. In no time at all, I was packed up and on my way here."

"Why didn't it scare you like that before; when you saw her by the sitting-room window?"

"Then I was merely the fascinated observer, hardly believing what I was seeing. Scrooge put it down to undigested beef, didn't he? It was rather like that with me – I put it down to mature-cheddar. This morning was different. Immeasurably different! I was face-to-face and spiritually involved with her. She was so young. We both were! Incredibly young and youthful again! I felt myself being lifted and drawn towards her as though she had some kind of claim on me!"

Dee sat up on the bed, now full of hidden concern and gently fingering the beads of perspiration from his brow. "Well, it's quite obvious to me that it was the long, lost Edward Barker she was claiming, not you. There's only one person making a claim on you, Guy Anderson, and she's here, living and breathing beside you right now!"

Dee swung her legs round from the bed and reached for the bedside telephone. "Hello there! Room service? Could we possibly have some more coffee and a strong pot of jasmine tea in the Minton-room, please? Yes, of course I mean now!"

69

"Now then," Dee said, grimacing into her tea-cup at the dregs, which were anything but jasmine. "I've sat here, like a doubting-Thomas, listening to what you are telling me; and summing it all up, Guy, this sceptic is now ready to accept that the cottage is quite possibly haunted by this unfortunate woman you call Mary Ann Barker. By discovering the grave, you've already proved that she did exist and you say you've already spoken to some old fellow who knew of her existence back in the forties. So, I suppose when you consider the tragic news of her husband's death, followed by her own untimely death in childbirth, it's perfectly feasible that the poor woman has become an earthbound spirit. As a Christian, I am not going to dispute the possibility of there being a spirit world, but…"

"But what?" Guy asked, stifling a yawn.

"But I'm not so convinced that you are the reincarnation of her husband. I'm afraid I find that very hard to swallow."

"I'm not surprised! I find it hard to swallow myself!"

"As far as I can make out, Guy, the only foundation you have for such a belief is the initial feeling of déjà vu, which you experienced when you first went there."

Guy sighed impatiently. "How many times do I have to say it, Dee? There's much more to it than that! I shrugged off the déjà vu almost immediately, but I can't shrug off the rest of it. Take the dream for instance; whatever could have motivated such an incredible insight into a hitherto unknown wartime disaster?"

"Well, with the knowledge that Edward Barker had been a wartime pilot who was killed over Germany, it's easy enough to see that your subconscious mind could have been elaborating on it, whilst you slept! It could be all those tales you've heard that have influenced you. Let's face it, everyone knows the strangest and weirdest things happen in the most ordinary dreams!"

"But Dee, this was no ordinary dream! It was terrifyingly realistic to the point of knowing that it was something that I had actually experienced! I lived and died in that dream! Now, I'm convinced that I've lived and died before!"

"What else can I say then, except that you haven't convinced me? I can't believe, Guy, that you have had a past life; not on the basis of a dream!"

"I wasn't dreaming this morning when I saw Mary. I was wide awake and bad dreams, ghosts and the like couldn't have been further from my mind. I was more bothered by the fact that you had driven off in a huff. I wish to God that you had stayed if it was only to witness what happened next. Can you possibly imagine what it's like to turn and see the ghost of someone you feel that you've known and loved? Not from this life, but from some past era!"

Dee was now looking resigned and thoughtful as Guy continued. "That's exactly how it felt, Dee. She was there! As clear to me as you are now! Her face was radiant with recognition. I could hear her voice as I'd heard it a thousand times before, and though we were feet apart I could feel the enormous energy and power of her embrace surrounding me – and Dee, it was in those few seconds that I knew I'd been on this earth before!"

"Guy, you really are obsessed, darling. Good God, it's almost as if you're under some kind of enchantment!"

"Obsessed – possessed – enchanted – call it what you will! I wish to God that it would go away!" He rose from his chair and walked into the centre of the room to stare up at the crystal pendants of the chandelier.

Dee joined him there and held onto his hand. "It will go away eventually. You'll see. The mind can concoct the strangest thoughts and ideas from a handful of coincidences. In our profession, Guy, perhaps we are a little more vulnerable because we spend much of our time acting out scenes of pretence and fantasy."

"It isn't fantasy! I can see her now!" he muttered, mesmerized by the faceted reflections of rainbow light dancing down into the pupils of his dark eyes. "She's wearing that pretty frock with the sweetheart neckline."

Dee was suddenly struck by the way he was uttering outmoded descriptions. *Frock? Sweetheart neckline?* Odd that it all came out so naturally.

Guy continued with his mind's eye view of Mary. "Her hair is swept up above her ears with diamante slides. She's so young and very pretty. A dead ringer for the girl in the snapshot."

"What snapshot?"

He turned quickly in her direction, jolted by her question. "Of course, the snapshot! I must show you! It's in my jacket!" He rooted quickly through the pockets and came up with the scruffy brown envelope. "How could I have forgotten to show you this, Dee. If you want proof, here it is! The best bit of evidence I've got – thanks to old

George – he found it amongst his mother's belongings. It's rather tatty and small, but it's a photograph of the two of them, taken in nineteen forty-one; he must have been home on leave at the time." Guy took out the small, grey photograph and handed it to Dee, pointing out the handwriting and the date on the back.

Dee peered over the top of her spectacles to scrutinise the uniformed Edward Barker standing smartly to attention with wife Mary on his arm. Wetting her index finger, she tried to smooth out the surface crease across their features. The coating of spittle seemed to do the most amazing things; especially to the man's face, which became strikingly clearer. A sudden sharp shiver riveted down Dee's spine. There was something so oddly appealing and sensitively familiar in that youthful and heroic expression. It could have been Guy. Startled by the revelation, she thrust the snapshot back into Guy's hand and walked over to the bedside table to light another cigarette.

"If you require further proof, take a look at this…" He held out the flimsy squares of paper and she quickly scanned her eyes over the war-office telegram, signed and printed in black.

"Did you notice the date of Edward Barker's death?" he asked quietly.

A slight wave of nausea caused her to stub out the cigarette. "Yes. Nineteen forty-two" she replied quickly.

"And the precise date? That is the day and the month…"

"I know, Guy. It's your birthday. I was aware of that."

"Yes. He died on the day I was born. What were you saying about a handful of coincidences?"

They stared into each other's eyes for answers and silently shared their mutual conclusions. She nestled against him, finally submissive and quite unable to question him further. "I have to admit, Guy, it's quite extraordinary!"

"Isn't it just?" he whispered into the waves of her hair as his arms closed around her – and for some time they stood motionless in the middle of the room.

70

Guy eventually found his voice. "It must be getting very late!"

Dee glanced at her watch, followed by a double-take. "My God, Guy, it's quarter-to-three. I'm astounded!"

"Oh, Dee, I'm so sorry, darling, for keeping you up so late and for subjecting you to all of that."

Dee reached up to kiss him lightly. "My pleasure, hope it's helped."

"You know it has!" His hands slid over the crimson silk on her shoulders, down the sleeves to her wrists. "Thank you, Dee. For everything. It's true what they say about a trouble shared! I think I've found my soul-mate in you."

"Those words will be my reward. Thank you, Guy. Now, if we're going to give another riveting performance tomorrow night, we'd better get some shut-eye."

"I'm ready when you are." He kissed her forehead.

"Okay, lover – if you give me back my hands, I'll say goodnight." She released herself from his grasp and walked towards the door.

"Hey, just a minute," he said, stopping her in her tracks, "Where do you think you're going?"

"What do you mean?" she asked in a contrived innocence.

"Well, aren't you going to sleep here with me?"

"I'd love to sleep here with you."

"Well then…" he said, indicating the enormous counter-paned bed.

"Thank you, but no! I have a room of my own, remember?" She picked up her keys.

"I know you have a room, but…"

"I have a reputation to keep, and what's more important, Guy Anderson, so have you!" She kissed him lightly. "Well, don't look so gobsmacked – go and get some rest! I'll see you in the morning at the breakfast table."

"Let me see you to your room then?"

"Thanks, Guy, but I know the way to my room." There was a victorious glint in her eye as she swept off down the dimly-lit passage.

Guy smiled to himself as he watched her go. People were inclined to underestimate Delia Davidson, he thought. Up until now, he'd been doing it himself. How wrong can a person be?

APRIL COTTAGE

71

Guy didn't see Dee at the breakfast table the next morning. Instead, he left a note at reception to be delivered to her room to say that he would see her at the theatre that evening, and that he would explain after the performance over late dinner. He knew that she would be disappointed; she would have liked to have been included on this little jaunt down to the Cotswolds, but the almost irrational decision to go had been made in erratic haste at dawn – and he spared her the disruption of an early-morning phone-call since she'd be needing extra sleep after last evening's long stint together. By seven-thirty, he had left the hotel.

Cruising down the M5 towards Tewkesbury, even though he was tuned into the radio with the non-stop informative chat and drama, Guy was ever mindful of the ordeal of last-night when he'd been consumed with fear. If only Dee had stayed with him instead of going to her room, he might have been spared all those horrendous visions and voices that had hauntingly hovered over him from the moment his head hit the pillow. He'd been tired enough to sleep for a week, but sleep hadn't come. Instead, Mary Ann Barker was there. She had been with him in the Minton-room, beckoning to him and bewildering him with lost emotions. She'd been there with him for every waking moment, pitifully calling him to return to April Cottage. She'd been there grieving and weeping for him and worst of all, holding the foetus of their unborn child in her arms. When a sort of sleep finally washed over him, he only found himself back in the cockpit of the burning plane, and having to once again endure the perils of hurtling through time and space into that dark unknown territory we call death.

Thank God, this wasn't unknown territory. This wasn't the cockpit of a bomber-plane. He was in the driving seat of his beloved Jaguar, on a very pleasant April morning, motoring down beyond Tewkesbury to the place of his birth.

On his way down from the Potteries, he'd frequently questioned his motivation for this hitherto, unplanned pilgrimage; but now, driving along by the Severn towards the sleepy little village of his childhood, he knew he'd done the right thing. Mary wouldn't be following him here, she was many darkened years away at April Cottage, and soon he would hopefully be in conversation with the one person who may be able to pass on some kind of spiritual guidance.

Driving at a snail's pace past the old vicarage, Guy turned his head to take a backward glance at the stately old house, standing half within the shadow of the church, where he'd been born and bred. His rustic reminiscences were bitter-sweet and the nostalgia continued as he drove on through that hallowed place where every bit of Cotswold stone held a memory of some kind.

Not many people were about yet – and those that were didn't seem to notice the elegant blue car, with the homegrown celebrity at the wheel as it cruised unobtrusively through the narrow street of neat little houses.

Cranberry House, the parish dwelling-place respectfully and charitably reserved for the retired clergy, was at the end of the street and Guy began to wonder what kind of reception was in prospect. The Reverend Christian Anderson was undoubtedly going to be surprised by the unexpected midweek visit from his very famous son, whose fleeting appearances were usually reserved for those between-tour trips, late on Sunday afternoons.

Guy checked his watch. *Would pops be up yet? Was he going to be annoyed, or confused by this sudden intrusion into the pattern of his quiet*

APRIL COTTAGE

and orderly life? It certainly would be out-of-character if he was, but realising that his father, at eighty-five, wasn't getting any younger, Guy was only too aware of the effects age could have. He dreaded the day when he would arrive to find his father in a poor state of health; perhaps bedridden or unable to communicate. Guy's infrequent visits were always preceded by these feelings of doubt and anxiety of guilt and self-admonishment.

This time, his concern was short-lived. As he pulled the car to a halt alongside the neat hedgerow of Cranberry House, he was relieved to see the frail, yet stalwart figure standing half-way down the garden path in the shadowy morning sunshine, indomitably armed with a giant pair of pruning shears. Guy watched, unseen, from the car and he could feel his eyes watering at the sight of the white-haired old gentleman; tenacious as ever, tackling the thorny trailers of an untamed shrub. There was such quiet dignity beneath that old woollen cardigan with the shabby brown cords; such wisdom beneath that shapeless straw hat with its strip of black trimming. Guy swallowed hard and honked the horn. There was nothing wrong with the Reverend gentleman's hearing because he reacted immediately, though his eyes took a moment or two to focus as he peered over the top of his spectacles at the car before wandering with uncertainty down the path, assuming it was somebody seeking directions. As he neared the car, the driver was getting out and standing to his full familiar height and he soon realised that the flashing, broad smile on the other side of the gate belonged to his only son.

"Guy!"

"Hello, pops! Surprised to see me?" The gate opened and their handshake was warm and sustained.

"Surprised, my boy? I didn't expect to see you here today! Is the tour over?"

"No, not quite; I have to be back in Stoke-on-Trent again for tonight's performance. That's why I've come early. We finish the tour on Saturday as planned. How are you, pops?"

"I'm fine, my boy! Well this is indeed an unexpected pleasure!"

"You don't mind me calling on you like this then?"

"Mind? I'm delighted! Come into the house and I'll make some tea!"

As Guy followed his father's shuffling steps along the path towards the house, he was made painfully aware of the dwindling stature of the man. The man who had once walked so tall in grand and solemn procession, following cross and choristers down the aisle to preach with eloquence and style at so many distinguished congregational gatherings.

"The garden's looking good, pops. You've been busy!"

"Just a little, though it never looks as good as when your mother was alive. She was the gardener. I do my best to keep it tidy. She's up there looking down, you know! If something needs doing, she lets me know." He scraped his shoes diligently on the grating by the door before entering the house. "Come on in, Guy, and mind your head on the beams! Now then, do you want tea or coffee?"

"I'll have whatever you're having. Let me help you."

"No, no, I can manage. Sit yourself down and get comfortable, I won't be a minute." He went through to the small kitchen.

Guy looked around the room, which was crammed with all the things of his childhood; things that had once stood within the spaciousness of that lofty vicarage – and which now looked infinitely more endearing in these warmer and cosier surroundings.

"Have you had breakfast, my son?" His father was calling from the kitchen.

"No, but I'm not in the least hungry."

"What about a little toast?"

"Perhaps later, pops. A drink will be fine for now, thanks."

Guy sank into a generous number of patterned cushions on the spacious high-backed chair, levelling his eyes on the open rolled-top desk where that same old grinning schoolboy photograph of himself was ludicrously placed amongst an array of religious books and ephemera. The objectionable whiz-kid in the silver frame had always been given a prime position.

Nothing changes; here he was again, like an oversized schoolboy returning to the nest for a dose of parental comfort and guidance. *How pathetic can you get?* He screwed his head around the wing of the chair to see if that enormous family-bible was still on the side-table. *Of course, it is!* A beautiful item, ornamented with gilt clasps and embellishments, but it was the newspaper that Guy eventually picked up to peruse.

"Here we are." His father hobbled in, rather shakily, with the tea-tray. Guy rose immediately to take it from him, placing it onto the small occasional table in the middle of the room.

"Now, pops, you sit down and I'll pour!"

"Very well – but let it stand in the pot for a couple of minutes – I think we're in need of a good, strong cup!" He steadily lowered himself into the seat by the brass-cluttered inglenook and the immediate relief of resting was written into his lined expression. "Ah, there we are. It's good to sit down for a while. I soon get weary, these days!"

"You still have home-help, don't you?"

"Oh yes – Mrs. Dickens comes in most days; such a dear lady! I'm very fortunate, you know, Guy, very fortunate indeed! And now, of course, they bring me meals in three times a week!"

"That's good." Guy's smile concealed his feelings of abhorrence; the mere thought of his father having to rely on the charity of others rankled, but it was pointless trying to alter things – he'd persistently offered substantial sums, which would have ensured a much better lifestyle for his father, but the retired vicar had always magnanimously refused; mainly because, Guy suspected, feelings of hypocrisy prevented him from taking advantage of the fruits of Guy's profession since he'd always been vehemently opposed to his choice of career.

"You mustn't worry about me, I'm well cared for. I consider myself to be blessed with kindness. These lovely ladies are always popping in and out to tend to my needs. Only yesterday, Ada, God-bless her, brought me one of her Dundee cakes. You must have a slice shortly! There's too much for me. You remember Ada, don't you? She was an old friend of your mother."

"Yes, I remember Ada and I remember her fruit cakes! Is she still plump as ever?"

"Yes – plump as ever!" Christian chuckled.

Guy noticed that the television set was draped over with a piece of tapestry and surmounted by silver goblets with a well-filled Tantalus. "Don't you watch television, pops?"

"Very little, these days. Bothers my eyes. I still prefer the wireless!"

"Oh, that reminds me – I've been asked to do the cast-away spot on 'Desert Island Discs'. The recording goes out sometime next year! You'll have to tune in!"

"How interesting, my boy." He replied with a proud smile. "I hope I'm spared long enough to see it – next year, you say?"

"That's right! I wouldn't mind being cast-away on a desert island right now!" Guy grinned cheerfully but the trained eye of the old parson was quick to detect something behind the cheerfulness.

"I think you can pour the tea now, Guy. It will be nice and strong."

They drank the tea in a brief sojourn of silence with the gentle ticking of the clock for accompaniment. The mingled whiff of lilac and wisteria drifted in through the open doorway on a dust-laden shaft of sunlight.

"It's so peaceful in here" Guy said, contentedly savouring the moment.

"Very peaceful!" his father concurred with a smile.

Another lengthy pause followed before Guy leaned purposefully towards his elder. "You must be wondering why I've come here to see you so early in the day?"

"Whatever the reason, Guy, it's good to see you. I appreciate you coming so far to see an old man like me."

"Save your appreciation, pops. I'm almost ashamed to say I've come because I needed to talk to you – entirely for my own selfish reasons."

"Oh?"

"But I hasten to say that I haven't come to burden you with anything. I'm not in any kind of trouble. In fact, things have been going very well for me since…well, let's not talk about things that are best forgotten." Guy had spoken very little about Roxanne's bit of scandal-mongering to his father and he had no intention of letting it rear its ugly head now. "It's simply that, well…I'm here to take advantage of your spiritual guidance."

"Then I'm flattered, Guy – and a little more milk please!" he replied, holding out his cup.

72

Looking for answers, Guy topped up his father's cup with milk, not allowing himself further hesitation.

"What would you say if I told you I'd seen a ghost?"

"I'd be extremely interested!" the Reverend said, sipping his tea.

"I was hoping you'd say that. Do you believe that there are such things?"

"As a Christian, I naturally believe in the spirit life, though I've never witnessed anything like that myself – yet. Are you speaking of an earth-bound spirit?"

"Yes, I suppose I am" Guy replied, though he didn't truly understand the question.

"And you say you've seen a ghost?"

"Yes, unfortunately I have"

"Tell me about it…"

"I've been staying in a rather remote place, known as April Cottage. Have you by any chance heard of that name before? I was wondering if I'd perhaps been taken there as a child? It's about seven miles outside of Stoke-on-Trent, down a remote country lane, near a place called Whitemoor; a small hamlet with a church, set back on the hill."

"No, Guy. We always travelled south or to the West-country. Never been to the Stoke-on-Trent area in my life. Why do you ask?"

"When I first arrived, I experienced an incredible sensation of déjà vu. It was just like seeing something for the second time, although I was certain I'd not been there before! When I drove down that lane for the first time, I knew what would be coming around every bend, long before I saw it!"

"Ah but, Guy, there can be many explanations for that kind of thing."

"Yes, I appreciate that – and let me say that it didn't bother me in the least. I settled down into the place without a qualm. You know how I've always appreciated a certain amount of solitude – I thought I'd found the perfect retreat. That was, until things started to happen."

"Go on, Guy. Tell me all."

Guy described to his father how everything had been triggered off by the sounds of a grieving woman and how he'd consequently became aware of her presence within the cottage. The elderly gentleman continued sipping his drink whilst he listened attentively as Guy continued with a graphic portrayal of the strange dreams and occurrences to which he'd been subjected, before revealing how it had all tied up with the factual things he'd learned about the Barkers. Guy unburdened himself, baring his soul as he spoke of the visitation of Mary and the out-of-body experience, which had mystically drawn him so close to her. Finally, Guy handed his father the photograph and war-office telegram, confirming of the pilot's death, along with voicing his belief that he was now the living, breathing proof of a reincarnated being, once known as Edward Barker.

Christian reached for a large magnifying glass, peering through it over the top of his spectacles at the crumpled bit of paper. He muttered something about it being very interesting before taking a slightly longer look at the snapshot. A look of concern appeared on his face. "How much longer will you be staying at this cottage, Guy?"

"It's mine until the end of the week, but I packed my bags and moved-out yesterday. I'm staying at the hotel where the rest of the cast are staying. I thought that would be the end of it, pops, but last night was horrendous! It all happened again, in my hotel room! I couldn't believe what I was seeing and hearing! She was there in my hotel suite. It wasn't a dream. She was really there!" Guy was visibly shaken as he slowly continued.

"She was calling me back to April Cottage – pleading with me to return there, to her and her unborn child! I could feel myself being physically and mentally drawn towards her. I must have passed out because later, I found myself in the middle of the room. I lay there for some time before groping the carpet and finding my way back into bed. When I eventually fell asleep, I had that awful dream again! I know, without a shadow of a doubt, that I was at the point of death!"

"And at that point, you were awake again?"

"Yes, thank God. I even thanked Him that I was alive."

There was a long silence, during which Guy began to feel foolish and immature. His father was going to be either non-committal or he was about to give one of his reprimanding lectures. It didn't take much to recall those regular admonishments of boyhood days in the vestry for provoking bad examples in the chancel choir-stalls. Whenever there had been whispering and giggling behind hymn books during prayers, it was usually Guy who had been summoned to the vestry for a sermon.

Now, however, things were different and the Reverend Christian Anderson treated his son with a great deal more respect – and Guy certainly didn't expect the response that followed.

73

"On the night you were born, Guy, I remember sitting in the parlour at the vicarage. It was a cold, bleak night in October and your mother was upstairs with the midwife. Old Doctor Sadler was in attendance. In those days, fathers were not allowed to witness the birth, so for me it was a long night of waiting – and your mother was being so brave! They kept coming to tell me how well she was doing and that it wouldn't be long – but it *was* long, Guy! I think it was the longest night I've ever known!" Guy waited as his father took a long, thoughtful pause. "It was of course wartime and normally, being a padre, I would have been away at my unit, but under the circumstances I'd been relieved from my duty. As I sat waiting for the midwife to call me, I remember turning on the wireless to listen to the nine-o-clock news – and for some reason, I've never forgotten that on that particular night, it was announced that a squadron of bomber-planes had carried out a successful raid over enemy soil and had safely returned to base, reporting the loss of only one plane, which had been seen going down in flames, somewhere over Germany."

Guy's huge intake of breath was followed by a stunned silence before his father continued.

"As I sat there, anxiously waiting for the joyous moment of birth, I couldn't help saying a prayer for those unfortunate relatives who were going to have to face up to the tragic loss of their loved ones; the pilot and crew, who would never be returning. In that very moment of sadness, Guy, like a miracle from heaven, I heard the shrill cries coming from the bedroom and the midwife came bustling in to tell me that I was the father of a very healthy boy."

74

Guy's eyes were riveted to the floor in a fixed stare and the old clergyman was only too aware of what was going on in his son's mind.

"However," he went on to explain, "we must never rule out that life and death are full of unexplained coincidences, which are way beyond our own comprehension. Make of it what you will, Guy, but never lose sight of the fact that we are merely human!"

"Is this not all against your Christian beliefs?"

"Well, let's just say that you won't be the first person to speculate, Guy. The Hindu and the Buddhist religions of India have long held the belief that our souls are reincarnated from one generation to the next; and I must say, it's an inspiring thought! Perhaps that's why so many famous writers appeared to have some belief in the subject. Rudyard Kipling wrote convincingly of it in one of his short tales, and I believe that was called 'The Finest Story in the World'. There were others too; Longfellow, Browning, Tennyson,

Goethe, Masefield and – oh dear, I'm sure the list is endless! Over the decades, the subject has been discussed into the next century and after! The fact I can remember that single bomber going down on the particular night you were born is, I have to admit, very curious indeed."

Guy rose and walked to the open doorway, ducking to avoid the low beams. Both excited and stirred by what he was now seeing as a positive revelation of the truth, he wantonly breathed in the nostalgic scents of mixed blossom as his thoughts moved on ahead of him. There had to be a way of finding out; now that he had tangible confirmation that a plane had gone down on the night that he was born. If he began to look into it, officialdom would be able to find out the pilot's name from their records, and if it turned out to be Flying-officer Edward Barker, then he would know the truth. He felt that he was on the threshold of confirming a past life. *His* past life!

75

The old Reverend Christian Anderson had risen from his chair and had moved to stand beside Guy in the doorway. "What is more important about all this, Guy, is that you mustn't allow it to dominate your thoughts, otherwise you'll be in danger of it becoming an obsession! That would be a tragedy, just when you're at the pinnacle of your career. You are in a noble and useful profession. I must say it – a noble profession that has brought you considerable fame, so learn the lessons of recent months! Gullible admirers will hang on your every word, whilst the sceptics will be critical and may elaborate on what you're saying, blowing it all out of proportion; as they've done many times before to your cost!" The man of the cloth purposefully turned to face Guy. "If the gutter-press get hold of this story, they would make the usual trivia out of it. I can see the headlines now – and surely you're not into that kind of sensationalism?"

"Heaven forbid, pops!"

The two of the stood in the doorway, looking out. Theirs had always been a peculiar kind of relationship. Father and son had never been able to quite reach each other – until now. Guy had never felt so close to his father than he did at that moment and he'd certainly never had greater respect for what his father had to say.

"You're right, pops. I'd be a fool to open my mouth about this to anyone."

"Well, if I'm the only one you've told, then your secret is safe."

"There are two others…"

"Oh dear."

"It's alright, pops, I know I can trust them both. One is the production manager who only knows that the cottage is haunted, nothing more."

"And the other?"

There was a brief pause.

"The other is Dee. Delia Davidson. She's with me in the play. We're good friends and, in fact, we've become quite close. I'd like you to meet her.

"She's not likely to divulge any of this? – perhaps in the future?"

"Not a chance, she can be very discreet and values our relationship far more than I deserve!"

"Then I shall look forward to meeting her. Now come and sit down again and let us discuss this matter more fully." He wandered back to his seat whilst Guy returned to the armchair.

76

"Now then, it seems to me that you've managed to convince yourself that you have been on this earth before and you've actually come face-to-face with someone that you once knew in a past life. Such things, of course, seem to be impossible; but as Matthew said, *'with God, all things are possible'!* Even if we do accept that God had arranged for this doomed pilot to have another life in order to return as he'd promised, and that you have been singled out for the regeneration – what of it? You can do no more than accept the situation – go about your business regardless! *This* life is what matters now! Believe me, there's such little time, m'boy! In this life, every single moment is precious and should be savoured."

Guy was reminded of words he'd heard before. "Ours is not to reason why – ours is but to do and die!"

"Precisely!"

"I know you're right, pops – and it makes sense to try and eliminate the whole thing from my mind. That's what Dee said I should do."

"She sounds very sensible."

"She is, and I have a lot to thank her for in all of this, but none have helped me as much as you have today, pops. You're so much wiser than your son. You've made me see this thing in proportion to everything else. The only thing left bothering me is...how am I going to rid myself of the stranglehold that Mary Ann Barker has upon me? She believes me to be her long-lost husband and the father of her child. What I saw last night was too awful to contemplate. Am I to be haunted and pursued by her for the rest of my life? I thought when I left the cottage I would be rid of her, but it seems she can choose to follow me at will. She waits until I'm alone and then she calls me and I get this awesome feeling of belonging to her! I don't mind telling you, pops, it makes me fear for my sanity!"

"Evil spirits need to be exorcised! With the help of the Lord, I've carried out at least one exorcism with some degree of success – but it seems to me, Guy, that this Mary is far from evil. Frightening perhaps, but not evil. Hers is more of a restless spirit that needs to be at peace, and she's halfway there. You are the only one who can help her, and it will be for your own benefit too. You need to be at peace with yourself, don't you?"

Guy nodded, feeling like a child.

APRIL COTTAGE

"Now then, m'boy, this is what you will have to do…"

77

It wasn't easy explaining to Dee. She didn't take kindly to being excluded from his visit to the Cotswolds. The situation had been eased considerably when, later that evening, after they'd played the tour's penultimate performance at the Theatre Royal, Guy had justified his actions more intimately, over a late dinner. It was then that he'd told her of his next decision, which was to return to the cottage, alone, immediately after breakfast the following morning.

He had assured her that it was absolutely necessary, for his own peace of mind – and that before moving down to London, he should try to carry out his father's instructions for 'laying Mary's spirit to rest'.

Dee was more than consoled by his insistence that after doing so, he would never want to see the place again, and more so with his promise of her having his undivided attention from then onwards.

78

In search of the sombre quest, the following morning, along the narrow country lanes leading to the little hamlet, Guy was aware that it was just seven days since he'd first driven that way to April Cottage, though it seemed like half a lifetime. He drove around the bend where he'd met the tractor, grinning to himself as he recalled the ruddy-faced farmer's assessment of him; *'posh car, collar and tie job, with an accent to match. I'd know you cattle auctioneers a mile off!'*

Driving on with the solemnity of a funeral director at the wheel of a hearse, he passed through the street of houses with its single shop - and the church, whilst his thoughts were concentrated on the secret silence of the bramble-covered grave in that lower corner of the sloping burial ground. Her brief epitaph would surely be engraved on his memory for all time.

Would Mary ever rest in peace? It was certainly the object of the journey; this was the only thing that would ensure her leaving him in peace – but was he capable of doing what his father had told him to do? This was a growing concern as he neared the cottage, armed with nothing but mounting trepidation.

What chance have I got of laying a spirit to rest, when my own miserable spirit is failing me with every passing second? He switched on the radio for a little, light music – something to lift his spirits. He immediately switched it off again on hearing the hypnotic, orchestral sounds of a new musical, which was sweeping the West-end.

He cruised down the hill where on that first visit to the area, everything had struck him with familiarity. Now, the same drive down that wooded slope with its fantastic hillside view was familiar merely because of the recent visits. All too soon, he reached the turning for the narrow lane with its half-submerged signpost. The tyres crunched ominously over the gravel, coming to an uneasy halt where the five stone steps of April Cottage jutted crudely out from the hedgerow.

Guy, aware of the fact that he was dithering, switched off the engine, removed the key and began twisting it, nervously, within his fingers. Only God knows how long he sat there, replacing and removing it from the ignition as each surge of indecision increased his apprehension. It was fear alright! Fear of that hidden desire to take the pieces of his past life and put them together to find the truth. Fear because he continued to feel that he was being drawn towards the truth! Fear because he was just plain scared, as he was before. The longer he sat and thought about the situation, the more he wanted to turn the car around and get away. Finally, the key was in the ignition and the engine was purring, ready to depart. In the desperate bid to escape, his right foot depressed the accelerator with such strength that his own weakness was being challenged by something reminiscently heroic. There was such intensity of sound as the revs increased and he was now no longer looking at his dashboard, but staring at a vastly and different, distinct set of controls within a violently shaking fuselage. He found himself calling to the rest of the crew to keep calm, though it was clear that those poor souls in the rear turrets had already been silenced. Now he was falling, hurtling down through roaring flames and searing heat. Then silence. Nothing but the black and lifeless silence of brave human ash, scattered within the confines of that grey silhouette of twisted metal. Not a living soul stirred on that wide stretch of charred pastureland. Not a living soul – except the solitary, transparent figure that arose out of the broken cockpit, drifting down from the wreckage and hurriedly dispersing into the distance of that foreign field, in search of a quest to find Mary again, even if it took him until the end of time. Simultaneously, Guy arose from the Jaguar with that same resolve.

79

Wandering down towards the cottage, which loomed like a silent cenotaph, hailing his return, Guy saw the beckoning shadowed outline at the sitting-room window as his feet involuntarily carried him along the pathway. He heard the echo of rippling, girlish laughter as the great key turned in the lock. The warped, old front-door, which usually needed a hefty push, swung open with ease as though someone had been there to open it. The sitting-room door was slightly ajar. He wandered in, drawn by the aura of light by the window – a light that was stronger and brighter than sunlight – a light that chose to fall upon the slender shape and form of a young girl in a pretty frock – a light that gleamed on strands of lustrous hair, drawn up at the sides with decorated clips.

Guy breathed in the exquisite fragrance and noiselessly spoke her name.

"M a r y!"

There was a sudden magnetism as he'd previously experienced, drawing and uplifting his disorientated senses out, and above a motionless, shell-like body – a body that chose to remain impassive, as some inner voice spoke to him:

"This is who you are – Edward Barker. Guy Anderson is merely a character from some strange scenario; his part has been played."

80

Mary's smile was radiant across her ghostly figure. She was now surrounding and rejuvenating Edward's released spirit with her closeness until they had merged into a single dimension.

Time was rapidly rewinding itself and everything was clearly defined. It was all there! The elation of that brief burst of happiness in their young lives when they had first come to April Cottage, newly-wed and crazily in love. Their untold joy was complete – that was, until that fateful morning in October, when he'd driven away in the black Austin-seven to join his squadron at base for a routine night-time sortie over foreign soil. As he'd left the cottage, he'd turned half-way down the pathway and seen the lone figure with a bravely tearful face at the sitting-room window. They'd finally waved to each other as he'd reached the gate.

"No goodbyes, sweetheart" he'd said cheerily, as he'd left the room. "No goodbyes, because I'm coming back to you. To both of you – and that's a promise!"

The repossession of his soul was already glaciating within the cold-storage of her spiritual caress. Would this feminine fortress of young and enduring love now hold and subjugate Guy forever? Not if that wildly pumping heart and mind within the form of flesh and blood below him had anything to do with it. *Yes, you were Edward Barker once, but not now! Not anymore! For the love of God, man, he was blown to bits decades ago!* The out-of-body response to the force of human gravity was immediate. Guy was almost on the point of rejecting his whole existence, but in a sudden, crystallising moment he knew there was only one existence to be rejected, as he recalled the words of his father.

"The reason you have to return to April Cottage, m'boy, is to say goodbye!". These pragmatic words had been gently persuasive. "Restless spirits, like this one, long to be freed from their anguish; in this case, it appears to be the vain anguish of waiting for someone to return. If you truly believe yourself to be that person, then with God's help, you have it within your power to end her anguish by assuring her that you have indeed returned, at least spiritually, as promised. Assure her also of the love that was once hers that she may now go in peace to that far greater love, which passes all understanding."

With his natural talent for memorising lines, Guy's chant-like oration of his father's words began, but the increasingly feeble utterances trembled and stumbled from his lips so unconvincingly that they were soon diminished to a stifled whisper – and despairingly, any further efforts to make an impact on Mary faltered to a halt. Had he imagined for an instant that he could act his way out of this one?

81

Ice-cold fingers were running through his hair and down the full-length of his spine. This time, it wasn't just his soul she was claiming – this time it was his body. Inch by inch he could feel her creeping presence enveloping his petrified limbs. The pervasive, aromatic fragrance hovered and lingered tantalisingly as her cold lips brushed against his. Like the touch of a butterfly's wing, her eyelashes flitted provocatively over the dark bristles on his face, settling on the lobe of his ear.

"Edward, my darling man! I've been waiting for you for so long!" It was a tremulous whisper; capricious, yet intimately prolonged – and it mingled with the strange distortion of sounds in the atmosphere as one half of him sought frantically to escape, whilst the other half merely languished in the aura of light that surrounded them. The violet, pink and silvery-white epicentre where her face, with its yearning expression, beckoned to him from beyond the grave. She was calling to him through the mists of time until he was being fleetingly drawn back through the past decades; time on the threshold of fame; time with the sultry Roxanne who'd claimed fifteen years of his life; time with long-forgotten school-friends in a Cotswold classroom; time as a toddler, being taken by the hand down the length of mosaic tiles on the church aisle; time as a baby, safe in his mother's arms and time as a foetus, safe in the womb.

The regression continued into a spherical tunnel of blackness, spiralling out before him as he floated, weightless, along its seemingly endless void. All his senses were fixed on that ominous light, which glimmered menacingly in the distance, but a lifetime away. Then, it happened. It was Edward who was letting go. It was Edward who went floating on towards it. It was Edward who was losing control and allowing himself to be manipulated by the touch, feel and smell of all things beautiful, bright and familiar. It was Edward who was wandering ever backwards into the youthfulness of a bygone era, where a long-lost love awaited him.

It was Guy who was struggling to return.

82

Shunning the strange faces, weird voices and effigies now exuding from the walls of the tunnel, Guy managed to find his own voice.

"Edward loved you, Mary. I know that now, beyond any shadow of a doubt – he loved you – and he loves you still, because love never dies! Not real love, like that shared between you and Edward! I could tell you about the kind of love that dies, but it's not a pretty story. I'd rather tell you about the love that lasts longer than life itself – and I have a chance of that too, now, Mary."

The aura of dwindling life had moved to the centre of the sitting-room. Mary's form could no longer be seen, but he knew she was still there.

Guy continued with a voice full of emotion. "You were with him when his plane came down, Mary. He saw your face in the clouds. I know this because *I* saw your face in the clouds! His sole concern was for you and your baby. Edward walked away from death to find you again, Mary! I was merely the vehicle for his quest, that is all.

The long years of waiting are over for you now. Edward has finally returned."

The only response was silence – and the only light in the room was shed by the morning sun. Guy's father had said that speaking to the unseen was rather like praying in the sense that although the response is negative; you know, through faith, that someone is listening and taking notice. Guy's own traumatic experience of speaking to the unseen had been more reminiscent of playing to a darkened audience beyond the footlights. Perhaps the chosen callings of father and son had not been so diverse after all.

"I have to go now, Mary." His words were swallowed into the heart-rending silence of the room.

Was this to be his closing-line? His final curtain? He stood motionless in the doorway, staring at the phantom-like shadows in the room. It was like standing in the wings after the performance – craving for another chance to go on, feeling that his audience might not have grasped his interpretation of things, filling him with reluctance to leave. Guy wanted to walk away, but there was still something lamentably lacking, leaving him feeling that his role was not quite finished.

83

Guy stood at the bottom of the cottage stairway, midway between the two closed doors with the front-door just off its latch; temptingly near enough for him to push open to make a quick departure. He sat down at the foot of the stairs, unable to make sense of it all. What an ordeal he'd undergone in that small sitting-room only minutes ago. His mind was turning over the moments of horror when that frightening magnetism had held him in its rigid grasp; its wanton power taking him further and deeper into oblivion. Mercifully, he'd fought against it with an inner strength and a relentless belief in all that he was striving to do, but was Mary now at peace with her beloved Edward? Was her soul at rest?

He had the strongest feeling within that his role was still not complete. There was no euphoria or sense of achievement to give him that peace of mind, which would have sent him happily on his way from April Cottage. It was essential to have that piece of mind. It was essential to know that

APRIL COTTAGE

Mary was no longer here, but he did not have that satisfaction.

He listened intently for any sound that suggested she was still around. All he could hear was the beating in his own temples – but before long, there were footsteps. Footsteps approaching. Guy was temporarily gripped with fear, before the earth-shattering relief as he realised they were coming from outside, towards the slightly-ajar door. Guy sat bolt upright on the stairs, not wanting to see anybody. He still had a job at hand.

"Hello? Anyone home?" a shrill, female voice called out. The voice rang out over the incessant tapping. Guy remained seated on the third step of the stairs, hoping whoever-she-was would go away – but then there was a kind of silent reassurance; a calm resilience; an acquiescence that in some strange way seemed to be in alliance with the arrival of the ignoble caller, and it was that sixth-sense that eventually drove him to the door.

"Good morning – do forgive me for intruding like this but, this is April Cottage, isn't it?"

"Yes?" Guy replied, keeping himself well within the confines of the passage.

"I just knew it! It's exactly as I've always pictured it!" she said, stepping back a pace as she stood, silhouetted by the sunlight. She pushed her sunshades up into the greying streaks of her hair to gaze up, admiringly at the yellowing brickwork of the cottage. She was tastefully dressed, with the jacket of her cream-coloured suit draped casually over her shoulders. The fact that she appeared to be an attractive, mature woman of considerable breeding didn't alter things as far as Guy was concerned. Whoever she was, her intrusion was totally disruptive and annoying to him at that moment in his precious time.

"You must forgive me for staring at your property like this, but I'm totally fascinated!"

"It isn't my property, madam" Guy said, ungraciously, making little effort to hide the fact that her enthusiasm for the place didn't concern him.

"Oh, I'm sorry, I naturally assumed…"

Guy interrupted. "I've had the place on private rental for a week and I'm now in the process of leaving. I was just saying goodbye to someone, so if you don't mind…" He made a move to close the door.

"I'm so sorry to have inconvenienced you – we shall have to come back at a less inopportune moment. I should explain that my daughter and I have travelled quite a considerable distance to see April Cottage. It's a kind of pilgrimage, you see.

APRIL COTTAGE

This cottage happens to be my birthplace. I was born here, back in nineteen forty-three."

84

Guy couldn't utter a sound. He simply stood, hovering at the half-open doorway, staring at this unsuspecting woman in the arched porchway, as if she was some kind of celestial being.

"You were born here? In nineteen forty-three?" he uttered, slowly.

"Yes – now I've given my age away, haven't I?" she said, breaking out a nervous smile. "Until quite recently, I didn't even know this place existed. Sadly, I never knew my parents. I know my father was in the R. A. F. but unfortunately, he was killed in the war. My mother died soon after I was born and I was adopted – end of story, I suppose."

"End of story?" Guy said, vaguely, as he continued to stare at her from within the shadows of the cottage interior.

"Well, not the end of the story if my daughter has anything to do with it! She's more excited about all this than I am. She's the one who's been doing all the research on my parentage. Normally, I'm not one for digging up the past but, I have to admit, I'm getting absorbed into it and now, as in a fairy-story, I'm stood here looking at this enchanting little cottage – my birth place!" She paused for a moment before continuing. "Look at me, rambling on. I will leave you to vacate the cottage and me and my daughter, Mary, will return later."

"Mary?"

"Yes, my daughter – she's in the car. I know it's an old-fashioned name but, it was my mother's name. Mary Ann…"

"Barker!" Guy interjected, stepping out towards her from the shadows of the passage.

"How on earth did you know that? She asked, incredulously, scanning the lean, dark features now confronting her. "Wait a minute, don't I know you? Have we met?"

"I don't think so."

"Haven't I seen you on a photograph? Are you a relative? My goodness, your face seems so familiar to me, I feel certain I've seen you somewhere before!"

"Well, I do get around a bit, but…"

Suddenly, her face lit up with a smile. "I know what it is! I'm mixing you up with someone else! You bear an uncanny likeness to that well-known actor – oh what's-his-name? You know, the fella that was on television the other night –

Anderson! That's it! Guy Anderson!" She laughed capriciously. "You must have been told that many times before! You even talk like him!" Then the truth dawned and was in evidence on her lively expression. "My goodness! You are him! Aren't you?"

His whimsical expression said it all. "Not much point in denying it."

This newfound knowledge changed her whole attitude. "My goodness, what must you think of me – chattering on about myself like this? Boring you with the details of my family history! I had no idea who you were…"

"What difference does it make who I am? You came here to see the cottage."

"I did, but I didn't expect to see a famous celebrity on the doorstep!"

"Fame has its price, so I opt for out-of-the-way places to avoid people."

"I can understand that – so I'm going to get out-of-your-way right now and let you get on with your personal goodbyes! Please give my apologies to the person you have kept waiting!" She hurried back along the pathway towards her car. Guy watched her, then started panicking. He couldn't let her go like that; her roots were entrenched into the foundations of April Cottage as much as his; he had to know more,

"Hold on a minute, don't go. Please, bring your daughter up to see the cottage. I don't have to leave for the theatre just yet – I could show you both around?"

85

Moments later, the lady visitor was walking back towards him.

"I happen to have a photograph of your parents. It was given to me by old George; a neighbour from down the road. Here…"

Guy handed her the small, grey snapshot. Pushing up her sun shades into her hair once more, she stared at it, unbelievingly. He noticed the unsteadiness of her fingers as she took it from him. He pointed out the inscription and date on the back but she only wanted to gaze at the couple whose brief moment of ultimate happiness was clearly captured on that two-inch square of film print. There were tears in the corners of her eyes when she turned to face him.

"How absolutely wonderful it is to see this! This is the first time I've set eyes upon my parents. I've often wondered what they looked like."

"It isn't very clear; a little bit worse-for-wear, but if you saw old George's place down the road, you'd wonder how it could have survived at all!"

"I just can't believe what I'm looking at!" She smiled, totally absorbed with the snapshot! "I can't believe the extraordinary likeness! Mary must see this – and she'd love to meet you! Would you mind awfully if I call her to come and take a look?"

"Please do, I'd love to meet her" he said, quietly.

As she picked her way down the lane steps to the lane, Guy was wondering what would happen if he told them that in another life, he was the man in the photograph. What would she think if he said, 'in a past life, I was your father'? He knew what she'd think – she'd think someone had been tampering with his brain.

Guy stood at the gate, watching her walk towards an open-topped sports car at the end of the lane. He could see that a young woman was seated at the wheel. Hearing her mother's call, she swung out a pair of stunning, brown legs with feet sporting a pair of trendy white trainers, and she wasted no time in reaching for her camera from the back seat to make a jaunty approach towards her excitedly beckoning mother.

As she came nearer, Guy was having to hold onto the gate-post for support; every ounce of colour had drained from his face. He was looking at a pretty girl in tangerine shorts and shirt; he was looking at a fresh-faced beauty with golden-blonde hair loosely piled onto the top of her head with long, straggly strands breaking free and falling to her shoulders, mingling with the coloured beadings that fell from the lobes of her ears. He was looking at a youthful, radiant smile that he'd seen before. He was looking at Mary Ann Barker.

"Mary, darling, you're not going to believe this! You're in for the most marvellous surprise!" They'd now reached the top of the steps to face Guy. "This gentleman just happens to be staying here at April Cottage!"

"Guy Anderson! It can't be! Not here! I don't believe it! Are you really staying here?"

Guy nodded, still unable to control his thoughts.

"You've got to be on a provincial tour, hanging-out in a place like this! You are, aren't you? Doing a play? I read about it being due for the West-end." She giggled, infectiously, holding out her hand.

"Hi!" he responded, holding onto the warmness of her hand to calm and convince himself that this young beauty of a girl was undoubtedly Mary in the flesh. "Forgive me for staring at you, but…"

"Grief! I'm the one who's staring! One doesn't expect to meet one of our most-famous actors in a remote hang-out like this!"

"And one doesn't expect to meet…" he stopped in his tracks, not saying what he intended to say, but nothing could stop him from giving her another searching look.

"What's the matter? Have I got spots or something?" she giggled again.

"I think I can explain why Mr. Anderson finds you so fascinating, Mary" her mother explained. "He can see the astounding likeness between you and my mother. Am I right, Mr. Anderson?"

"But you don't know what your mother looked like? You've never seen her!"

"I have now. We *both* have. Take a deep breath and have a look at this. This was taken back in the forties in this very garden…"

Mary grasped it in delight. "Grief! Are these two who I think they are?"

"Who else can they be, darling? You only have to look at the young woman to know – she's the image of you!"

"I suppose she is" she said, eagerly scrutinising the snapshot. "This is incredible! Where did it come from?"

"It belongs to Mr. Anderson, Mary."

"I've already explained to your mother, Mary, old George gave it to me" Guy chipped in, now beginning to feel that he'd already known the two of them for years.

"Old George?" Mary questioned.

"He's certainly getting on a bit, but he's a likeable character who lives down the lane. I was asking him about the history of the cottage. He told me about the Barkers and their tragic circumstances." The older woman was now gazing wistfully over the blossom-strewn garden. "Apparently, during the war, whilst your father was away, George told me that his mother befriended your mother and she was actually here when you were born; giving the midwife a helping-hand. Years later, George found two things in her belongings; that photograph, and this…" He held out the official notification of Edward Barkers death. "It might be too painful for you to see, but I suppose it would have been infinitely more painful for your mother to have seen it when it arrived here on her doorstep in nineteen forty-two."

She cast her eyes over officialdom's grim message before passing it on to her daughter, who was anxiously waiting to see it.

"I hope I haven't distressed you too much" Guy said, gently touching the older woman's shoulder.

"On the contrary," she faced him with a certain pride in her eyes, "you have given me the strongest link with my past than I could have ever hoped for. You've given me something tangible to hang on to. How strange that you should happen to be here at this moment in time, just when we came along." Her words faltered for a moment. "Surely it has to be fate, Mr. Anderson?"

"Please call me Guy; everyone does. I can only say that 'there's a divinity that shapes our ends, rough hew them how we will'"

"Shakespeare?" she responded quietly.

"Hamlet!" the younger girl added, breezily swinging her camera into action and levelling it at the cottage. "And talking of Shakespeare, mother, Anne Hathaway's cottage has nothing on your birthplace; not a thing! No tourists for one thing, and another – it's genuine!"

"Why do you think I chose it? Not for its five-star qualities, I can assure you" Guy intervened.

"I know exactly why you chose it, Guy" Mary went on with enthusiasm. "This place still lives and breathes – it positively oozes with the past. I can feel it! Thank God, we've managed to see it before some whiz-kid decides to give it a face-lift with a sandblaster and double-glazing. Can you imagine this place in the winter, with icicles hanging from the window-ledges and a strong east-wind lifting the ivy from the roof; and snow drifting up from the lane, packing itself against the doorway and blocking you in for days at a time? You'd feel so cosy and warm within those walls, wouldn't you?" She reached out her hand to touch the corner of the house, finding that the crumbling brickwork was warm from the sun's rays. "It could have been a day like today when my Grandparents came here to begin their married life together. We know that it was April. That is why they renamed the cottage."

"They re-named it?" Guy queried.

"Oh, yes!" she exclaimed brightly. "I've been doing my research. Apparently, this dear little house was once known as 'The Larches'. I don't know why when there isn't a larch to be seen! So, Edward and Mary renamed it April Cottage because it was April when they moved in. It's also why my mother was christened 'April', isn't that right, mother?" Her mother merely smiled with exuberance.

"I'm sure Mr. Anderson isn't interested in all this, Mary."

"You're wrong! I'm more interested than you would ever know. So, you were christened April?"

"Yes, my adoptive parents were told that it was the last word my mother said before she died. Consequently, I was given the name because it was her last wish."

APRIL COTTAGE

"Your adoptive parents must have been very nice people."

"They're wonderful people; they've always been so open and honest with me. I love them dearly."

"May I take a picture of you, Guy?" Mary said, moving closer to him with the camera.

"Of course – where do you want me?

"That'll do, just in front of the porch. Hold it…cool! Now, just one more please. Do you mind if mum stands with you for this one?"

"That's enough, Mary! Whatever must you think of us, Mr. Anderson?"

"The name's Guy, April, now come here and stand with me and let your lovely daughter take a picture of us! I think it will make Mary very happy!" Guy wasn't talking about the Mary holding the camera.

"Smile, please! …Gotcha!"

"Come on, darling. We must leave Guy in peace now, I insist on it. It really is too bad of us to delay him any further, especially as he has someone waiting in there to say goodbye!"

"Oh, I'm so sorry, I didn't realise!" Mary joined her mother in preparation to leave.

"Look…" said Guy, wanting to explain, "I know the press have been giving me a bit of a murky reputation of late, but if you think I've got a woman in there, you can forget it. Instead, I have a confession to make – in fact, there's no-one in there. It was just a ploy I was using to get rid of someone I thought was an over-zealous fan, or a tedious gossip-columnist. Believe me, they are always intent on breaking down the barriers of one's privacy. I do apologise, April. I hope you understand."

"I see," she said, lowering her sun shades and giving him a provocative little smile. "And which category was I put into – the over-zealous fan or the tedious gossip-columnist?"

"I suppose you think I'm a pompous ass!"

"Not likely! We are both avid admirers and understand that you must get sick and tired of being hounded."

"I'd love to have hordes of people following me around!" Mary said, diving beneath the apple tree to take an upward shot of the blossom. "I'd survey the thronged masses with utter contempt and cast a carefree eye in the other direction before sailing lazily off into the sunset, on my yacht!"

"Do you seriously think I have that kind of lifestyle?" Guy asked amusedly, watching the girl swinging her camera around in all directions.

"Mary is never serious, Guy. If you look closely, you'll see that she has a very mischievous glimmer in her eye. I don't know where she gets it from. It certainly isn't me or my husband!"

"Tell me about your husband…"

"He farms. Mainly fruit-growing these days. We have a lovely place down in Kent; loads of orchards and an old out-house complete with a ghost!"

"Ghost, eh?" Guy said, unflinchingly.

"Yes – now you'll think me absurd! It's supposed to be an old coachman, but nobody's ever seen him. It's rather nice to have a mystery about the place, don't you think?"

"Grief!" Mary called out in the process of taking another shot of the cottage. "I thought you said there was no-one in there?"

"There isn't" Guy replied, hastening towards her.

"Well I've just seen a woman at the window! She was looking directly at me and smiling!"

"She couldn't have been. There's no-one in there!" Guy said, sounding a little too anxious for his own good.

"But – I had her in focus through the lens of my camera – just for an instant, but when I looked up, she'd gone."

"It must have been a trick of the light or something." Guy offered.

"Are you sure there's no-one in there?" she asked quizzically.

"Not a living soul!" he insisted, realising his words implied the truth. Next, he came out with something that, he hoped, offered an inspired explanation. "I can see what's happened – you've been looking at a reflection of yourself in the window. Look, if I stand here, I can see myself quite clearly – that must be what you saw through the camera."

"Yes, of course, Guy. That must have been it." There was that mischievous glimmer in her eyes as she moved closer to him, lowering her voice. "Don't worry, my lips are sealed."

86

Mary went to join her mother on the pathway to look at the cottage. Soon they would be gone and Guy would probably never set eyes on them again. The thought disturbed him as he stood by, observing their intrigue with the place and their fascinated expressions as they tried to peep through the open doorway to get a mere glimpse of the interior. Mary was taking a final camera shot as he walked towards them.

"I'm sure you'd like to see inside before you go? I warn you, though, it's fairly primitive in there; I just happen to like extremes."

April's face lit up and she was on the point of accepting his invitation, but her daughter gave a discreet little cough and mumbled something about it being more tactful to return later when they wouldn't be intruding.

"Yes, darling, I think you're right! Guy has already given us too much of his time – it wouldn't be fair." She turned to him with a polite, yet decisive expression. "This has all been so exciting for me – for both of us! We're truly grateful. You have been very kind and accommodating and your time is bound to be taken up with so many commitments. We must have been a bit of a pain dropping in on you like this when you're in the process of leaving."

Pain? They had no concept of the kind of pain he was experiencing at that moment. It was a pain of incalculable frustration, brought on by the threat of their imminent departure. It was fast becoming clear to him that all three of them had been mystically drawn to April Cottage for a reason; why else should their visits have coincided? This was destiny, not coincidence. Why would they be lingering together at the open doorway with a mutual belonging for the place – not to mention the presence within? Guy had no intention of letting them go – not just yet.

"Who I am and what commitments I have are irrelevant. I absolutely insist that you see the inside of the cottage before you leave, after all, this *is* the place where you, April, first saw the light of day. How can you possibly refuse to enter and take a look around?"

Without waiting for a reply, he took hold of April's hand and took her through the small passageway into the living-room. "This little room, Spartan though it might be, has been my home for a week. Pity the fire isn't lit; you could have seen how the place comes alive with its glow!"

Mary followed them into the darkened passage and glanced suspiciously at the closed sitting-room door. "Grief! What a hoot!" she exclaimed over her mother's shoulder. "Look at that fireplace! Wow! Look at that table and those chairs – it's like stepping back onto the celluloid of a thirties film! What's behind that curtain?"

Guy grinned. "Take a look – it's all mod cons in there with any amount of cold water on tap. You have to boil the kettle over the fire to get hot water, so I'm afraid I can't offer you morning coffee."

"Mum, come and have a look at this old stone-sink!" Mary hollered, enthusing her fingers, reaching to explore the thick lead piping, crudely battened to the brick wall above the single tap.

April was too absorbed with the framed print over the mantelpiece. "Prepare to meet thy God" she whispered, inaudibly.

"Strange you should be interested in that; there's something written on the back that I think you should see." Guy reached to take it down. "I happened to be taking a look myself and carelessly dropped it and shattered the glass." He passed it across to her, indicating the hand-written inscription on the back.

"Mary! Come and have a look at this, darling!" April called. "It will interest you; it's signed by Charles Barker!"

Hearing the name, Mary's appearance from the pantry was immediate. She clutched the print eagerly, taking it over to the window to get more light.

"It belongs to you now, Mary. I know that he would want you to have it."

"But I can't just take it!"

Guy gave her a singular look. "Don't worry, I'll see to it that the landlord gets his price. I'm sure it won't mean much to him. Consider it to be a gift from me on behalf of your great-grandfather.

"How can I refuse?" Mary said, staring at the print with a possessive smile.

"You must have these as well!" He handed the small snapshot and the telegram to April."

"This is so kind of you!"

"They belong to you. Now then, would you like to see upstairs? Feel free to wander – the rooms are very basic, but extremely quaint."

"All of this seems so unreal to me" April said, obviously overcome.

Not half as unreal as it all seems to me, Guy thought, as he escorted her to the bottom of the stairway.

"Are you coming, Mary?" April called.

"No, mum, you go up there and have a quiet little look on your own – I know emotion when I see it!"

"Thank you, darling. I know I'm soft, but now that I'm actually here inside the cottage, I have this profound sense of – oh I don't know, it's hard to put into words."

"A sense of belonging, perhaps?" Guy asked, watching her going up the stairway.

"Yes!" April concurred, turning to face him as she reached the top. "That's it exactly! A sense of belonging!" She smiled at him before disappearing into the dinginess of the bedroom.

"My mother will never forget this, you know! Until recently, she never talked about her real parents and at first, she objected when I started delving into things, which is understandable, I suppose. I always expected, however, that she wanted to know more about her roots – and coming here today has made me realise that I was right." Mary looked out through the open doorway to the garden. "You have been so welcoming and kind! One wouldn't expect someone famous like yourself to give a jot for the likes of us!"

"Oh, believe me, Mary, I'm as interested in all of this as you are!"

"You couldn't possibly be, could you? I mean, you must have seen the grandest places on Earth! Why would you be interested in an insignificant little place like this?"

"I've been staying at this cottage for the past seven days, remember. You cannot stay here for too long without realising there's something very special about April Cottage. Like your mother says; there's a sense of belonging. It's because of that sense of belonging that I believe these walls once embraced a very real and powerful love – a love that still exists today!"

"I can see why you're an actor of repute, Guy! You said that with such vision and feeling, you've sent shivers down my back!"

"I wasn't acting, Mary, I meant every single word!"

"Oh, I know you weren't acting. Your eyes were full of sincerity." She gave him a curious look. "Tell me, what is this powerful love? What love? Whose love?" The triplet of questions was fired in quick succession.

"I think you'll come to know what love I'm talking about."

"Really?"

"Really!" he said, noting the look of fascination that she had for the sitting-room door. He diverted her attention to the garden once more. "It's just a sitting-room through there and I haven't been doing too much sitting in it. It's not as cosy as it is in here – in fact, it's damned cold in there! I wouldn't bother going in if I were you."

"Don't worry, I won't. We'll be off in a moment when my mother comes down" she said, lowering her voice, confidingly. "It's not on, you know – keeping her waiting in there if it's cold!"

"What? Keeping who waiting?"

"Your lady-friend! Oh, come on! I know she's in there!" Her eyes twinkled mischievously as she turned her face into the stream of sunshine at the porch-way. "Don't worry, I shan't breathe a word to anyone!"

"Do you really think I've got a woman in there?"

"Yes! I saw here – at the window, when I was in the garden!"

"You *think* you did!"

"I know I did! But not to worry, it's nothing to do with me or anyone else! Your private life is your own as far as I'm concerned."

Guy wondered if he should let Mary go, believing that he had a woman secretly hidden away. Keeping that door shut would probably be the wisest thing to do if the ghost of Mary Ann Barker was still manifesting itself within those walls – but his hand was already on the doorknob. Suddenly, he felt a surge of energy that was drawing him to open the door and usher young Mary into the room.

87

The door almost swung open itself and Mary wandered in, a little warily, into the centre of the room where she stood gazing intently around the plain white walls with its small latticed windows, before turning to face Guy with another mischievous grin.

"She seems to have done a bunk!"

"I can't convince you, can I? What you saw was your own reflection!"

"Alright! I believe you – thousands wouldn't!" She emphasised the cliché with a smile then rotated her eyes, in a more pensive mood, around the four corners of the room. "You're right about it being cold in here!" she said, visibly shivering. "It isn't just cold – it's deathly cold!" Suddenly, she heard April coming down the stairs. "We're in here, mum – in the cold storage department!"

April appeared at the doorway, staring into the room with an almost disorientated expression.

"I can't explain it," she said, "but I seem to be getting the strangest vibes within this cottage.

It's almost as if someone is here – listening and watching as we speak. Forgive me for asking, Guy, but are you sure there is no-one else staying here?"

Ignoring the daughter's whimsical expression, Guy aimed his rather direct response towards her mother. "What do I have to say to convince you both? Let's get this straight – I'm not in the habit of having illicit affairs in country cottages and hiding my loose women in the closet! It's not my style. I have a very lovely lady waiting back at the hotel. Perhaps you've heard of Delia Davidson? I will shortly be joining her there before we go off to do our final performance for a Potteries audience. Tomorrow we'll be driving down to London – together! Does that answer your question, ladies?"

April hastened, blushingly, to give her apologies. "I feel so embarrassed. Forgive me, I didn't mean to…"

"Please don't apologise. After all, it was me who put the initial idea into your head that someone was here. I simply want to establish that I'm staying here alone."

"Of course! Forgive me – I wasn't trying to pry. I too wanted to establish that you were staying here on your own so that I can come to terms with the experience I've had just now in the bedroom. It was a kind of strange elation – I was acutely aware of a comforting presence." She gazed at the small snapshot in her hand, her fingers caressingly positioning it onto the framed print she was carrying where the flimsy squares of thin paper had fallen apart to reveal the black printed word of death.

Guy felt a wave of passion sweeping over him as she gave him a tragic, yet polite smile. She suddenly seemed so fragile and vulnerable and he longed to grasp her by the shoulders, look into her eyes and say *"I know all about your mother! She was very pretty, youthful and fresh-faced with a fair and stunning figure, lively, iridescently gorgeous and so very much more – and here in your daughter, she lives and breathes again! I can tell you how deeply and passionately she loved your father and how terribly grief-stricken and alone she was when he was killed – and how she lost her will to live without him – but then her anguished soul refused to rest and she has waited for more than half-a-century for him to return. I could tell you about your father too, April! Oh yes – I could tell you so much about Flying-Officer Edward Barker, who has finally returned to his beloved Mary, just as he promised all those years ago – and he is here for you now, April. I can assure you of that!"*

Guy knew that none of this could be said. He could only stare remorsefully at this woman who had stepped so briefly into his life. He knew he could never divulge any of it to her or her daughter.

This lovely woman, of some breeding with such an educated and cultured demeanour, was his own age. The two of them must have been born within days of each other after that fateful plane crash, which had resulted in his own, previous death.

So how could he ever say the words? *I was your father, once. That fallen hero on the snapshot was me! The lovely young girl was your mother and my beloved wife. Minutes before you and your daughter arrived, I was communicating with her in this very room. I can feel the aura of her presence encompassing us. You can feel it too, can't you, April? I can tell by the way you are engrossed with those small mementoes in your hands. If you look across at your daughter – you will see that she too is utterly preoccupied with the revelation – see how her lips are slightly parted; how her eyes are twitching as she gazes into the living light...* "Oh, my God!" Guy exclaimed inaudibly as he suddenly snapped out of his inner monologue, realising just how the great fixation was in the young girl's eyes. Mary was now in a deep trance.

88

Every nerve in Mary's body had become static and the pupils of her eyes were deeply aligned with those of the apparition, which had obviously chosen to make itself visible to her.

Guy, having been there before, recognised the situation at once. He knew, without a doubt, that it was Mary Ann Barker's ghost manifesting itself again; this time, to her unwitting granddaughter! He couldn't let this happen! His worst fears were that the girl was now undergoing the same kind of out-of-body experience that he'd had himself. Was she being mystically drawn into the powerful aura of her grandmother's affections? A grandmother who had already made a convincing contact through the lens of Mary's camera?

Was this young, innocent girl now being possessively lured, as he himself had been lured, to that eternal place beyond the grave? Judging by the rigidity and deathly white pallor of her countenance, she was!

Guy was immediately relieved to see that April, hitherto unaware of her daughter's preoccupied state, had gone over to the window and was staring out over the blossom-strewed garden with its endless array of sprawling weeds. He was even more relieved when something out there had captured her attention to such a degree that, mercifully, without a backwards glance she was hurriedly excusing herself and hurrying out of the room, delightedly muttering about not having seen one of those for years. Whatever had captivated her must have been prearranged by some angel of mercy.

"M a r y!" he whispered anxiously, to the girl and touching her gently with no response. "Come on, Mary, we have to leave now; your mother is outside in the garden waiting for you" he said, even more coaxingly. "I have to lock up the cottage now to leave for the theatre – MARY!" He was beginning to panic; the girl's breathing was irregular; there was such dangerous, profound expression in her eyes and he didn't like the way her lips were drawn up into a tight little smile.

"I know that you can see her!" he said with an urgency that rasped at his breath. "I've seen her too! It's your grandmother, Mary Ann Barker, isn't it? You have to let go, Mary! For God's sake, and mine, let her go!" He glanced anxiously towards the window. April was returning, slowly and euphorically along the garden-path, holding a cluster of small, pink flowers. Somehow, he had to prevent her from coming back into the cottage; she must not be allowed to discover that her normally vivacious daughter was in some kind of soporific stupor. The only way was to go out there and join her on the pathway, thus stalling for time. Hopefully, Mary would eventually come out of the trance.

He was already out in the passage-way when he heard the young girl's voice ringing out to him like a clear bell on a frosty morning.

"Wait, I'm coming with you!" she trilled from the innermost confines of the sitting-room.

"Thank God!" Guy uttered with relief, hurrying back to lead her out of that fateful room – but he was devastated to see her arms outstretched in the other direction.

89

"No – NO!" he called out in desperation. "Don't go with her!"

Mary's voice trailed, uttering the two syllables in 'goodbye' in soft monotones. Guy was agitated almost out of control; he was on the verge of praying for the young girl's deliverance with the deepest kind of concern as he moved closely towards her. He stood in front of her, holding her hands very gently with tears welling in her eyes and a faint, natural smile was hovering at the corners of her mouth as she again whispered goodbye.

"Mary! Come back to me, Mary!"

Mary was now looking at him directly and he let go of her hands.

"Are you alright, Mary?"

"Yes, I'm alright. She's leaving us now. She's going farther and farther away from us. Guy was immediately pacified to hear Mary speak with such calm serenity. "She was smiling at me as she went – I can't hear the voice anymore. Perhaps she can hear mine? Goodbye, my dear grandmother!"

Mary walked a step forward and then turned to Guy with a radiant expression. "I know who you are. I know what you have been through. It's all clear to me now. My grandmother, she showed me – like a dream! You're free, Guy - She's gone. She's really gone! I can't smell her perfume anymore, can you?"

No response was necessary from Guy. The assurance was clearly there. They were two people on the same wavelength. She put her hand into his outstretched arm and allowed herself to be led out into the sunlit garden.

90

"Look, Mary, darling, Myosotis Sylvatica – Rosy Gem. I've not seen these pink forget-me-nots for years. We had enormous amounts of them in the garden when I was a girl. They're growing in a clump over there in the midst of all those weeds. I couldn't resist pulling-up these few little roots to take home. I shall be able to plant them out and have a permanent reminder of this very special day in my life – the day I returned to my birthplace – and the day I met Guy Anderson!"

For the next few moments, the delicate pink petals of the forget-me-nots became the focal point – a kind of mystical symbol of their union. Each had their own thoughts, and as if to endorse the mutual thinking, April broke off two sprigs of flowers, handing one to her daughter and the other to Guy.

Very soon now, they would be making their farewells and going their separate ways, but each would be leaving with a new awareness of things that might have been.

Before leaving, Mary approached Guy and beckoned him close, whispering in his ear. "Don't worry, I meant what I said – I shan't breathe a word to anyone!" She backed away and shot that mischievous smile at Guy, accompanied by a wink of solidarity. Guy nodded towards her in quiet appreciation, as the mother and daughter prepared to leave.

"We must never lose sight of each other!" Guy called after them as the open-topped sports car began to move swiftly away.

"We won't! See you in the West-end from beyond the footlights!" Mary called out, cheerfully waving a hand in the air."

"See you both in my dressing-room, after the show!" he called in reply.

"You're on!" April yelled as the car drifted out-of-sight at the end of the lane.

91

Guy made a brisk return down the garden path to pick up the key from the cottage. For him, there was nothing left. April Cottage was merely a place – an empty, dingy little place waiting for a face-lift.

The massive iron key was firmly slotted into the gaping key-hole and was turned by him for the last time. Removing it, he clutched its cold, inanimate weightiness in his hand and strolled away down the path towards the wicket gate. Before descending the five stone steps, he turned to look back one last time. There was no face at the window and no-one waiting at the door. Suddenly, bathed in the glow of April sunshine, it seemed to be a very ordinary little cottage and he saw no reason for ever wanting to return.

On his journey, back to the Five Towns Hotel, he stopped the car, parking alongside the row of red-bricked houses on the hillside hamlet of Whitemoor and wandered down to that deserted corner of the little churchyard. Pausing for a moment whilst he realigned himself with reality, smiling to himself as he took in all the events of the past week, before placing his sprig of forget-me-nots upon a certain grave.

92

"Guy, why are we taking the M5?" Dee asked from the passenger seat of his car the following morning.

"Because," Guy replied, "this is the way to the Cotswolds…"

"Why the Cotswolds? I thought we were going to London?"

"We are, but we're making a diversion. I want you to meet a certain gentleman. My father."

"Your father! How lovely, Guy! Will he mind us calling in on him like this?"

"He's expecting us. I rang from the hotel last night."

"Why didn't you tell me?"

"I wanted to surprise you."

"So, that's why you arranged for my car to be driven down to London!" Dee smiled.

"Yes. I'm taking you both out for a splendid Sunday-lunch. He's looking forward to meeting you, Dee."

"And I'm looking forward to meeting him! How wonderful, Guy! What a lovely surprise!"

She gave him a radiant smile and contentedly reached for her cigarettes. Guy gave her a sidelong look of disapproval.

"There's just one thing, Miss Davidson – if you and I ever get to the altar, you're going to have to give up smoking. I want a good, long and healthy relationship!"

A packet of menthols went sailing swiftly through the car window, sprinkling an array of gold filter tips onto the slow lane.

APRIL COTTAGE

EPILOGUE

New York, USA
April 1991

"Oh, Guy, it's so beautiful!" Dee exclaimed, looking at the large diamond on her finger. The two newlyweds were sat drinking morning coffee in the honeymoon-suite of New York's famous Waldorf hotel. The past year had flown by. "Delia Anderson!" she pronounced proudly. "Oh, I think I'm going to love being Mrs. Anderson!" Dee continued repeating her new name like an excited child on Christmas eve. "HEY! Are you listening to me, Guy?"

Dee's words were oblivious to him. He was far too involved in the entertainment sections of his newspaper as he sat, cross-legged on the opposite side of the table.

"Guy Anderson! Talk to your wife!" she demanded.

Guy suddenly snapped out of his bubble. "I'm sorry, darling – I'm just reading *this*. Have you seen it? It's all about our big day! It seems that

Guy Anderson and his lovely new wife are back in favour amongst the press and the public!"

"No way! Let me see!" Dee shot off her chair onto his lap, pushing herself in front of him; eager to see their latest publicity and reading-aloud as she perused the article:

The Anderson Marriage.

America's favourite adopted actor, Guy Anderson, got married for the second-time last week to the beautiful Delia Davidson. It was a low-profile affair as the two were wed in a small church in the village of Whitemoor, England – a place shrouded in secret sentiment for Guy and Dee – sentiments they refused to reveal to the press! Guy brought his father, the Reverend Christian Anderson, out of retirement for one day to conduct the service, as guests were limited to a handful of friends of the happy couple. One guest; a local man known as George Smith, commented on his delight to receive an invitation to the celebrity-wedding, exclaiming Guy Anderson to be 'a true scholar and a gentleman'. Due to the low-key nature of the event, we were unable to gain much insight into the big day, but one cryptic comment from the groom left us wondering just how much Beaujolais he'd consumed: 'Today, I am born again into new life. May I be the first to raise a glass to the happy couple, who will remain together forever, in this life and the next: Here's to Edward and Mary!"

Dee shot Guy a reprimanding smirk, before stating "well, I think that's lovely!"
"Oh, that's not all, dear – continue reading…"
Dee picked up where she'd left off.

With Guy Anderson's popularity soaring, we caught up with his ex-wife, Roxanne, who was the first to be voted-off the trashy reality-tv show 'Celebrity House' this week. It's fair to say that it has not been a good year for the disastrous diva – firstly being publicly dumped by her young toy-boy, followed by her inability to land any starring roles. When asked about her feelings towards the marriage of Guy and Delia at an interview following her eviction from Celebrity House, she embarrassingly threw a tantrum, wrought with expletives, before storming off-set.

Dee's laughter was hearty, from the stomach. "Well, you can't say she didn't have it coming!"
Guy sniggered.
"Everyone has their comeuppance in the end, Guy! Everyone!"

"I really don't care, Dee. I have no feelings towards her one way or the other. I wish her all the best, but the only woman *I* care about is the beautiful Delia Anderson" he said, emphasising her surname.

"Oh, Guy – you really *are* a scholar and a gentleman – and *you're* the only man *I* care about – and I always will – forever – in this life, and the next!" She winked at him with her tongue in her cheek.

Guy stood up from his seat, lifting Dee as he went, cradling her in his arms. "Now then, Mrs. Anderson..." Guy threw her on the bed and proceeded to pull the curtains shut. "What say we shut out the world beyond you and I and have a little *us* time?" Dee giggled playfully, welcoming him with open arms as he climbed on top of her...

...and somewhere thousands of miles away, in an unseen dimension, Edward and Mary Barker stood hand-in-hand, smiling upon them.

APRIL COTTAGE

Printed in Poland
by Amazon Fulfillment
Poland Sp. z o.o., Wrocław